KIDNAPPED

BOOK TWO:
THE SEARCH

GORDON KORMAN

KIDNAPPED

BOOK TWO

THE SEARCH

SCHOLASTIC INC.

New York   Toronto   London   Auckland   Sydney
Mexico City   New Delhi   Hong Kong   Buenos Aires

For Daisy

ISBN-13: 978-0-439-84778-0
ISBN-10: 0-439-84778-8

16 15 14 13 12   11 12 13 14/0

Printed in the U.S.A.   40

First printing, July 2006

PROLOGUE

Welcome to the Blog Hog
News, Opinions, and Whatnot
www.bloghog.usa

When the FBI wrongly imprisoned Doctors John and Louise Falconer for treason last year, they made a terrible mistake. But that was only the beginning. After the couple was released, no one even considered that a family denounced and defamed as the worst traitors in fifty years might be at risk.

Now we see the result. Four days ago, eleven-year-old Margaret Falconer was kidnapped and is being held for two million dollars' ransom. And the FBI's botched rescue attempt yesterday only places her in greater danger.

When is the Bureau going to stop jerking these poor people around? They were found innocent and deserve protection as much as any other citizen. Why is Emmanuel Harris, the man who arrested the Falconers in the first place, still the lead agent in this case? It's time for the authorities to get serious before that little girl winds up dead. . . .

1

The trunk of the kidnappers' car. Location: unknown. Destination: unknown. Time: unknown.

Meg bounced around, trying not to hit her head on the trunk lid each time the vehicle went over a bump. She felt like one big muscle cramp. The pain was bad enough to make her forget what was happening to her—that she was at the mercy of ruthless criminals who might decide to kill her at any minute. She had, after all, seen their faces.

How long had she been locked in here? Too long. It had to be at least fifteen hours. The first light of dawn was beginning to filter in through the airholes drilled into the trunk lid. In all that time, she'd had no food, no water, and no opportunity to get out and stretch. If she didn't find a bathroom soon, she was going to explode.

No, she thought. *Bathrooms can wait.*

Now that she could see again, she had to take stock of what was in the trunk—anything she might use to escape from her captors.

The most obvious weapon was a metal tire iron. A crude plan took shape in her mind. She could bash at the trunk lock until the lid popped. Of course her captors would probably hear the banging and put a stop to it. Then she'd lose her tire iron and her chance. Bad idea.

She rolled onto her side to investigate what, if anything, was deep in the back of the trunk. There was a set of broken jumper cables, an ice scraper, a dried-out sponge, an empty yogurt container, and — what was this? A small box of ammunition for a pistol, .38 caliber. She overturned it, and two bullets dropped into her hand. She sighed. Useless by themselves. Unless —

In addition to his career as a noted criminologist, her father, Dr. John Falconer, was the author of a series of detective novels. In *The Gun That Never Was*, the hero, Mac Mulvey, solved the mystery of a shooting with no firearm and no ballistics markings. Mulvey realized that a sharp blow on the back of a shell casing had the same effect as the hammer of a gun. It ignited the gunpowder, which set off the bullet.

She could fire these shells if she could hit them hard enough with the tire iron.

She struggled to recall the details of the book. Dad's writing was on the cheesy side — all wild action, not very memorable. One thing stood out, though, in Meg's memory: It was impossible to aim precisely when you were shooting this way. If she tried, she could end up doing herself far more harm than good.

But as the wave of disappointment washed over her, her eyes fell on the wheel wells that made the trunk so tight and uncomfortable. If she could shoot out a tire, her captors would suspect nothing more than a blowout. And then . . .

She took one of the bullets and held it like a nail against the rounded wheel well on the driver's side. She hefted the tire iron —and immediately chickened out.

I'll probably blow my hand off!

If she couldn't keep it steady, she'd never be able to hit in the right spot.

Then the morning outside brightened, and a shaft of light from one of the airholes drew her attention to the sponge. Excitedly, she pressed the bullet into it, leaving the back of the shell exposed. To her delight, it stood firmly on the wheel well.

Gingerly, Meg got to her knees so that her back was pressed up against the underside of the trunk lid. A tremor of fear ran through her as she raised the tire iron. She always felt this way before trying something from Dad's books. Mac Mulvey was fiction, and this was all too real. If she somehow put this bullet into the gas tank, it would be curtains for all of them.

Maybe I shouldn't . . .

It was the hesitation that convinced her. Meg's brother, Aiden, was the timid one in the family. He thought fifty times before brushing his teeth. Meg's strength was action.

Do it!

The edge of the tire iron slammed against the shell. She felt the impact all the way up to her shoulder. The bullet did not fire.

Come on, Dad! Tell me you didn't make it up!

She was aware of raised voices inside the car. That meant they'd heard the noise. With any luck, her captors had put it down to the tires kicking up a rock against the undercarriage. But she couldn't expect to get away with twenty tries at this. There weren't that many rocks on any road.

This has to work — fast!

She raised the tire iron once more and concentrated on the target like a karate master about to split a stack of boards.

Pow!!

The smell of gunpowder filled the trunk, choking her and burning in her nostrils. The bullet tore down through the wheel well and ripped into the tire. The blowout made an even bigger explosion. A split second later, the car was reeling all over the road as the driver fought for control.

Meg was knocked violently around the confined space. *What have I done?*

Just when she thought they'd either swerve off the road or into oncoming traffic, the driver regained control and the sedan limped to a halt on the soft shoulder.

Behind the wheel was a burly, bearded man with a gruff voice and a personality to match. Meg had dubbed him Spidey because of the Spider-Man mask he'd worn on the day she'd been taken.

"What next?" he roared. "A flat tire! Why doesn't anything ever go right?"

"Is there a spare?" the kidnapper Meg called Mickey asked nervously. At twenty, he was the youngest of Meg's captors, nicknamed for his own disguise, a Mickey Mouse head.

"There'd better be," intoned the third occupant of the car, the only woman. She had also been incognito during Meg's abduction — in a Tiger Woods mask. Meg called her Tiger.

Spidey, Mickey, and Tiger. The Three Animals.

They didn't bother to hide their faces any longer. By now, their captive knew them all too well. It was just another foul-up in an operation that had seen more than a few.

And now this blowout . . .

Mickey got to the trunk first. He popped the latch and peered inside.

The tire iron swung up and slammed into the side of his head.

The blow was so hard and so completely unexpected that Mickey dropped like a stone. Meg vaulted out of the trunk and hit the pavement in a full sprint. By the time Spidey and Tiger came after her, she'd turned her head start into a thirty-yard lead. Mickey managed to scramble up and join the chase.

Meg took in her surroundings. She was pounding down the shoulder of a rural highway, bordered by chessboards of rolling farmland, dotted with distant cottages and barns. It was pretty country, but with no hiding places, no people to help her, no telephones for dialing 911.

How come you can never find a gas station when you need one?

A quick over-the-shoulder glance told her that her pursuers were gaining. She veered off the road and began plowing through a freshly tilled field, wincing at the overpowering fertilizer smell. It was a gamble—the layers of loose soil would slow her down, but they'd also slow down the kidnappers. Meg was betting that her fugitive experience would give her the advantage over rough terrain.

She bulldozed on, kicking up dirt with every footfall. Behind her, Mickey wiped out in a shower of mud and manure. She felt a twinge of regret at conking him with the tire iron, since he was the only one of her captors that she considered a human being.

Her lungs were an inferno, her breath a series of choking gasps, made all the more uncomfortable by the intense stench. Was the gap widening? Impossible to tell — she couldn't risk slowing herself down by looking backward. She didn't seem to be losing ground, but how long could she keep this up? Sooner or later, the kidnappers' longer legs would overtake her. The nearest farmhouse was still at least half a mile away.

She vaulted a rail fence and came down on the hard-packed sod of pastureland. As she scrambled toward a stand of trees, she caught a glimpse of movement — a coffee-brown coat, a large animal shape, head down, grazing.

A horse! Meg's spirits soared. With any luck she could hop on and ride it bareback to the house. She raced around the grove.

And froze.

The creature that stood before her, eyeing her with flared nostrils and an unfriendly glare, was no horse.

It was shorter, broader, heavier, and definitely meaner. Powerful muscles rippled beneath the bull's smooth hide. It was already pawing the turf and snorting, its massive head lowered. The horns looked like spear points.

It amped Meg's panic up to a new level. Her kidnappers meant her no good, but this was certain death.

The monster charged, and the ground rumbled. Without even thinking, she snatched up a fallen tree branch.

A fat lot of good this is going to do against those killer horns!

All at once, she remembered a TV documentary on bullfighting. The purpose of the red cape was to distract the bull away from the matador's body. Could a quivering leafy branch do the same thing?

She was about to find out.

Wheezing in terror, she hefted the limb, shaking it off to the left. To her amazement, the beast shot by, following the rustling leaves. Her breathless relief was short-lived as the bull wheeled around for another attack. This time the onslaught was coming directly at her.

Frantically, she swung the branch out to her right. At the last second, the animal changed direction and blasted into the leaves, its head jerking wildly. An overwhelming force wrenched the limb from Meg's hands and tossed it contemptuously aside.

Now unarmed, Meg scrambled up the nearest tree,

clawing the rough bark until her fingers bled. The bull charged again, slamming into the trunk just a few inches below her. The whole world shook with the impact—at least, that's how it seemed to Meg. She lost her grip and fell to the grass.

Dazed and spent, she could only squeeze her eyes shut and wait for the lethal horns to rip into her.

The devastating blow did not come. Amazed, she looked up to see the bull streaking away from her.

But how—why—

"Get away from me!" bellowed a voice.

It was Spidey! The burly kidnapper was barreling toward her—on a collision course with nearly a ton of rampaging livestock. He got within twenty feet before breaking off and hurdling the fence to safety.

Meg fled in the opposite direction. She made it about three strides before a mud-caked Mickey leaped out and grabbed her.

"Bring her here," ordered Tiger in the calm, merciless voice Meg found so chilling.

"Let—me—go—" Meg pounded her fists against Mickey's chest. But there was very little fight left in her. So many hours crumpled into a ball in the closeness of the trunk, followed suddenly by this frenzied bid for freedom . . .

A piece of white cloth flashed in Tiger's hand, accompanied by the sharp smell of chloroform. Meg was fading out.

"Aiden —" she mumbled.

It made sense that, at such an awful moment, her thoughts would turn to her brother. They had been fugitives together during their parents' imprisonment. Each had risked everything to save the other countless times.

But they weren't fugitives anymore. Aiden was a regular citizen in a regular house with a regular life. He couldn't come after her even if he wanted to. Mom and Dad would never let him.

I'm all alone, she thought.

Everything went dark.

3

Knight to bishop six.

Aiden made the chess move, wondering if he had gone totally insane. Meg was kidnapped—last seen stuffed into the trunk of a car headed God only knew where—

And I'm playing a game!

His opponent, Richie Pembleton, frowned at the board beneath the brim of his Greenville Cubs baseball cap. "It's a trap, isn't it?" Richie grumbled resentfully. "You're trying to sucker me."

Aiden rolled his eyes, exasperated. "Do you want to play, or what?"

Richie was highly insulted. "Of course I want to play. That's what friends are for—to support you through thick and thin."

It had been going on all morning: Richie badgering Aiden into match after match to take his mind off his sister—and then getting sullen and moody when Aiden beat him.

Doesn't he see that a hundred chess games couldn't take my mind off Meg?

A shadow appeared over the board, and Aiden nearly jumped out of his skin. Hard experience had trained him to be on constant watch for sudden and unexpected danger. It was a difficult instinct to turn off—even in the safety of his own living room.

But when he looked up, he found the friendly hobbitlike features of Rufus Sehorn. Sehorn was more commonly known by his website name, the Blog Hog. He had taken a personal interest in Meg's kidnapping.

"May I?" the blogger requested, sliding Richie's bishop along a diagonal of black squares.

"That won't do any good," Richie said sulkily. "He'll just take my knight."

"But you have a counterattack." Sehorn began manipulating the pieces on the board, demonstrating the moves of both players. "See?" Richie's queen sliced in for the kill. "Checkmate."

Richie was bug-eyed. He stared from the board to Aiden. "You never told me he was *smart*!"

Aiden, too, was impressed. But the blogger's presence meant much more than a chess strategy. Two days before, a ransom demand had been sent to www. bloghog.usa. It was still their only contact with Meg's captors.

"Have you heard from the kidnappers again?" Aiden asked anxiously.

"No. Nothing like that," Sehorn told him. "But I do have a piece of information about the case—"

Twenty feet away, John and Louise Falconer sprang up from the couch as one person.

"Rufus!" Mom cried. "What's the news?"

The blogger's expression radiated deep sympathy. "I'm sorry to get everybody's hopes up. The kidnappers haven't sent another message. The news I have concerns—"

The front door opened and in stepped a short, squat man in a suit that was a size too small. The Falconers regarded him quizzically. They were accustomed to the comings and goings of the various police officers and FBI agents assigned to Meg's abduction. But nobody recognized this newcomer.

"May I help you?" John Falconer prompted.

"Oh—sorry." The man held up a badge. "Mike Sorenson. I'm the new lead agent in the Falconer kidnapping."

"What happened to Agent Harris?" Aiden piped up.

"He's been reassigned," Sorenson told them.

It was a major shakeup. Harris was the agent who had arrested the Falconers in the first place. He had also arranged their release once they'd been proven innocent. He had pursued Aiden and Meg for more than seven thousand miles in their fugitive days.

He's almost like our personal agent, Aiden thought. For the FBI to pull Harris off the investigation meant they had to be furious over the failed rescue attempt.

"Maybe it's for the best," the Blog Hog offered gently. "A new approach, a different style. This was the news I was going to tell you."

Aiden regarded Agent Sorenson from top to bottom. Nobody could be less like Emmanuel Harris. The former lead agent was a towering six-foot-seven African-American. His replacement was a platinum blond and at least a foot shorter.

"Of course we'll do anything we can to help you, Agent Sorenson," promised Louise Falconer. "Would you like some coffee?"

"No, thanks," said the newcomer. "I don't drink coffee."

He's practically the anti-Harris, Aiden thought. Harris's coffee addiction was legendary.

Sorenson turned his attention to the Blog Hog. "You're Sehorn, right? The blogger? We think you might be able to help us."

That was another big difference between the two FBI agents. Harris did not conceal his dislike for the press — and for Rufus Sehorn, in particular.

"I'll do whatever I can," Sehorn promised.

"The government is offering a ten-thousand-dollar re-
ward for information leading to Margaret's rescue. We'd
like to use your website to get the word out. Of course
we'll use the regular media as well. But we know the
kidnappers have an eye on your site, since that's where
they sent the ransom demand. We want them to feel the
noose tightening."

Aiden couldn't keep his emotions from pouring out.
"But it *isn't* tightening! Ten thousand isn't so much! You
offered more than twice that for Meg and me when we
were on the run. What does that mean — law-abiding
citizens aren't worth as much as fugitives?"

Richie put a hand on his shoulder, but Aiden shrugged
it away.

"That's enough," his father said sharply. "We should
be happy the Bureau has finally sent us an agent who'll
get serious about rescuing Meg."

Aiden kept his mouth shut. He had no great love for
Harris. Yet Harris was someone they could trust. He had
nearly destroyed their family, but he had never actually
lied to them. In spite of all the misery he had brought,
he was a fair man. Even Meg would be forced to agree
with that.

Aiden's eyes ran over the creases and bulges of Sorenson's ill-fitting jacket. This unprofessional-looking rum-
pled mess now held Meg's life in his hands.

A line from an old book rattled disquietingly in Aiden's head: *There's always a rockier road than the one you're on.*

Yes, it was good to be rid of Harris. But what if his replacement turned out to be even worse?

4

Curled up in a ball in the car, Meg faded in and out of hazy consciousness.

I'll never get used to that chloroform headache. . . .

A short distance away, her captors were changing the ruined tire. Meg struggled through the fog to tune into their conversation.

"That's a bullet hole!" Spidey was saying. "We didn't run over a nail—she shot out the tire from inside the trunk!"

Tiger was impatient. "With what? The ice scraper?"

"Maybe she had a gun, but she pitched it while we were chasing her," Mickey suggested.

"Don't be a fool," Tiger scolded. "Why would she throw away a ticket to freedom?"

"Well, we searched the trunk and we searched her," said Mickey. "There was no gun."

Spidey vowed, "I'll beat it out of her."

"I won't let you!" Mickey exclaimed.

"You and what army?"

Tiger put a stop to the argument. "The last thing we

want is a damaged hostage. We should have expected something like this. She's tricky and she's resourceful. Remember, she and her brother had every cop on earth running around in circles. We've got to be extra careful with her."

"Tie her up?" suggested Spidey.

"Not good enough," Tiger told him. "We can't let her out of our sight for a second."

And so new travel arrangements were born. Meg rode in the car, with sunglasses and the visor of a baseball cap concealing her features.

At least I'm out of the trunk. This was an improvement. Sort of.

Beside her — crowding her against the door, in fact — was Spidey. The bulge in his jacket was unmistakable. His gun, pointed directly at her.

"Try something and I'll drill you," he vowed.

Meg took him at his word. In the days since she'd been taken, the burly kidnapper had alternated between rage and cruelty. He was capable of kidnapping; he was capable of violence. She had no doubt that he was also capable of murder.

The spare tire was a "doughnut," a temporary replacement to get the car to the nearest service station. Twenty miles down the road, the Buick pulled into a dilapidated garage with a hand-painted sign:

FUEL — MECHANIC — LOTTERY TICKETS

"Take her for a walk," Tiger told Mickey. "I don't want anybody to get a good look at her."

The youngest kidnapper was mystified. "Who's going to see her? We're in the middle of nowhere."

"*Him,* for one." Tiger indicated the coveralled mechanic, who was strolling to meet them. "These days, every grease monkey has ninety cable news channels and a high-speed Internet connection. This girl is a celebrity."

"Yeah," Meg agreed bitterly. "I should get a star on the walk of fame."

"Watch your lip." Tiger turned to Mickey. "Get her out of here — now."

"I have to go to the bathroom," Meg complained.

"Hold it in," Spidey growled.

"Forever?"

Tiger released an exasperated breath. "Give me the gun."

Concealing the weapon in her own jacket, she opened Meg's door and led her toward the small public bathroom beside the garage.

Meg weighed the possibility of conveying her plight to the mechanic. But how could she lock eyes with him when she was hidden behind sunglasses? He'd never even see she was looking at him. Maybe she could flip up the shades, just for a second—a silent S.O.S. She raised a hand to her temple.

Tiger read her mind. "You're putting that man in danger," she warned. "Do you want him to suffer for your mistake?"

Meg lowered her hand. It was bad enough that the Three Animals were prepared to shoot *her*. But an innocent bystander? Even a chance at rescue wasn't worth risking the life of another person.

The small bathroom had no windows and only one entrance. Still, Tiger examined it carefully before leaving Meg alone inside. "Be quick about it," she ordered.

The instant the door closed, Meg knew the clock was ticking. There was no escape from this tiny room. But maybe, just maybe, she could use these precious few seconds of privacy to send out a distress call.

She did an inventory, which didn't take very long. There was a sink and a toilet—not exactly cutting-edge communications equipment.

It came to her as she was about to flush. There might be a way. It was a long shot. No, to call this a long shot was an insult to long shots.

Her brother was the world's biggest fan of their father's novels. During those weeks on the run, it had been Aiden who had used Mac Mulvey's wild schemes to get them out of the direst situations. Meg had begun studying the books after the family's ordeal had ended. Hey, you had to stop being a doubter when there was proof the stuff actually worked!

If I do something from Mac Mulvey, there's a chance Aiden might recognize it.

In *An Education to Die For*, Mulvey is locked inside a restroom on the unused top floor of a New York City high school. He screams for help, but that only speeds up his breathing of poisonous gases given off by the toxic chemicals planted there. With time running out, the resourceful Mulvey finds another way to make his presence known. He moves along the line of stalls, clogging the plumbing with bathroom tissue. When he flushes, the overflowing toilets send a flood of water streaming out under the door into the building. A worried student reports a cataract cascading down the stairwell, and an investigating custodian frees Mulvey mere seconds before suffocation.

Feeling as silly as she was desperate, Meg removed the tissue roll, pushed it into the toilet, and inserted it directly in the drain opening. Next, she took the backup roll, wondering if she should unravel the paper into the water. That would fill the bowl with mushy cement.

No, she decided. *This has to be an exact copycat crime to have any chance of reaching Aiden.* Mulvey didn't have time to make cement. In that story, the clock was ticking as the air filled up with deadly fumes.

She stuffed the backup roll in whole.

There was a pounding at the door and Tiger's impatient "Let's go!"

She experienced a moment of panic. What if Tiger had to use the bathroom after her?

No time to think about that . . .

"Coming," she called brightly. And she flushed.

The plumbing made an unhealthy gurgling sound as the mushy pulp tried to jam itself through the drain. The water level began to rise.

Meg let herself out of the bathroom and closed the door behind her. "Thanks," she said to Tiger. "I wasn't feeling very well."

Message sent.

Twenty minutes later, the Buick passed a sign advertising a gas station two miles ahead. Meg, who had been complaining of a stomachache since the previous stop, doubled over in pain. "I need a bathroom!" she groaned.

"You just went!" Spidey snapped

"I have to go again! Please!"

"Oh, all right," Tiger said in annoyance. "But this is your last chance. Get yourself straightened away."

"I'll try," Meg sniffled.

This time there was only one roll, but it was the thick, extra-absorbent brand. It took all her strength to cram it into the narrow drain, while Tiger pounded on the door, urging her to hurry up.

The result was even better than before. The heavy mass of wet paper acted like a giant cork, quickly sealing the opening. She barely got out of there before the overflow hit the cement floor.

"Feel better?" asked Mickey back at the car.

"A little," she mumbled shyly.

At least until the next stop . . .

The trick worked twice more. Towns were few and far between on Route 119, a tiny two-lane road that wound its way west toward the Appalachians. But every time the signs told of a gas station, general store, or luncheonette, Meg's mystery illness returned. She would clutch her stomach and beg for another bathroom break.

"She's playing us," Spidey whispered as Meg faked sleep after the third stop. "Nobody goes to the bathroom this much."

"You do if you're sick," Mickey argued.

"She's got an angle," the burly man insisted. "She's marking her trail, leaving clues for the cops. Notes in lipstick on the mirror."

"She's got no lipstick, and there are no mirrors," said

Tiger. "These are Stone Age bathrooms, and she has nothing but the clothes on her back."

"She had no more than that when she shot out our tire," Spidey observed sourly.

"She had a bullet," Tiger countered, "because someone was stupid enough to leave live ammunition in the trunk."

"It isn't live unless you've got a gun to shoot it out of!" Although he lowered his voice, his frustration was evident.

"Well, she did it, so obviously it was more live than you think!"

Meg felt a small measure of satisfaction knowing that her captors were fighting over her antics.

If I drive them crazy enough, maybe they'll let me go.

If only.

On the fourth bathroom stop, she decided to be careful. Her kidnappers were growing suspicious. She doubted any of them had read Mac Mulvey. Still, a toilet jammed full of tissue rolls would look fishy if Tiger happened to check on her. So she took a single roll and packed the center cardboard tube with a crumpled paper towel. Then she got down on one knee and pressed it far enough into the drain so that it was out of view.

She had barely gotten back to her feet when Tiger pushed the door open and peered in suspiciously. Her narrow eyes tracked up and down the walls and floor, searching for any unusual markings. She found only random doodles and graffiti.

"I'm done," Meg told her.

"Then let's go."

And before following her onto the dirt driveway, Meg reached back inside and pressed the flusher.

She had sent Aiden four "messages," but what were they, really? Tiny glitches in a universe of plumbing. How many toilets blocked on a typical day? Thousands? Hundreds of thousands? What were the odds that her brother would hear about four of them?

She thought of him, hundreds of miles away by now, distant and remote. All at once, she felt ridiculous. She was the victim of a terrible crime — kidnapped, held for ransom.

And what am I doing to save myself?

Vandalizing bathrooms.

Reaching Aiden this way would take a miracle.

5

Aiden stared at the screen until the words on it became meaningless squiggles. The Blog Hog, CNN.com, the website of every newspaper he could think of. Every time he felt the impulse to shut down the browser, his arm would not respond to commands. The next screen, the next link might offer a clue that would help solve Meg's kidnapping. How could he rest before that happened?

He worked at his sister's computer rather than his own, hoping that something in her room might jump-start his brain. Surely there was a lead that the FBI hadn't considered yet? But every time he looked around, it was with a swelling sense of hopelessness and the horrible feeling that time was running out.

No one had the heart to clean up Meg's stuff since her abduction. Unfolded clothes oozed out of drawers; books and board games were jammed every which way. Meg's messiness had once seemed like an insult to Aiden's carefully ordered life. Now this place was sacred ground. When he stood here, he felt Meg's absence like a vacuum cleaner sucking at his heart. It was painful, yet he cherished the pain because it brought him closer to his sister. It made her real again.

His eyes fell on a stack of folders and work sheets on the edge of the desk. Meg's homework, sent over by her teachers. It was a show of support more than anything else. Of course Meg would be fine. She had all this catching up to do.

Nobody was bringing homework anymore, Aiden noted sadly. At this point, there was a very good chance that it would remain forever undone.

Focus! he commanded himself.

There were updates about Meg on the web, but they mostly rehashed the botched FBI rescue. They were sprinkled between stories of international events, celebrity gossip, and headlines as varied as AMERICA'S OLDEST BIKER STILL LEADER OF THE PACK AT 97 and DON'T TAKE AWAY PLUTO'S PLANET STATUS, SCIENTIST PLEADS.

People cared more about a lump of frozen rock than Meg's life.

His eyes fell on the silliest headline of all: THEIR BOWLS RUNNETH OVER — BATHROOM VANDALS HEAD WEST.

DINGLEY, VA: 6:19 p.m.—Somebody has a grudge against the plumbing along Route 119. In the space of barely three hours early this afternoon, vandals struck four consecutive public bathrooms on a stretch of this isolated rural road. The damage? Not broken windows or offensive graffiti, but four badly clogged overflowing toilets.

"It may not sound like much," said a local police spokesperson. "But that's every comfort station for a hundred miles."

According to police, the four incidents are "definitely connected," each with the identical M.O. — an entire tissue roll jammed directly into the drain. Even so, the department has no intention of going after the perpetrators. "We'll let Roto-Rooter take care of this one . . ."

Aiden snapped back from the computer as if he'd been slapped.

No, it can't be . . .

He reread the story. *An entire tissue roll jammed directly into the drain.*

Mac Mulvey? Could this be Meg broadcasting a secret distress signal via Dad's books?

Her life was on the line! If she got a chance to send a message, would she be crazy enough to waste it on blocked toilets?

All at once, he realized it was the *perfect* message. Something Aiden would recognize, but her captors wouldn't — not unless they'd read *An Education to Die For.*

He pulled an atlas down from Meg's bookshelf and threw it open, hunting furiously for a map of Virginia. There it was—the town of Dingley, barely a speck. And running right through it, Route 119, a winding farm road that meandered west from the capital region.

She'd been held on the Virginia side of DC. When her kidnappers fled town, they would have followed the last road anyone would be watching—something like Route 119! She'd be kept in the car, well hidden. The one thing they couldn't deny her was a bathroom break!

And she found a way to send up a signal flare.

His sister was one of a kind.

6

"**B**athroom vandals?"

John Falconer scanned the news story and then swiveled his laptop so his wife could see the screen.

"Don't you get it?" Aiden exclaimed. "Mac Mulvey did exactly the same thing in *An Education to Die For*! Meg knows it's something we'd pick up on. She's telling us where she is!"

"By blocking toilets," Mom said dubiously.

"They're not going to let her send a singing telegram!"

"Aiden," she admonished gently. "We won't bring your sister home with sarcasm."

"Nobody wants Meg safe and sound more than your mother and me," Dad said earnestly. "But we have to keep our heads. Criminology is our field. A clogged pipe isn't a lead. It isn't anything."

"Yeah, but four of them in a row?" Aiden challenged. "Along a road you'd take if you were trying not to be noticed?"

"You could say that about a hundred roads," his mother pointed out.

"If it's such a common thing, how come they wrote an article about it?" Aiden demanded.

She shrugged. "It's funny. It's a slice of life."

Aiden was stubborn. "It's Meg!"

"You're talking about an eleven-year-old girl," his father reminded him. "She's helpless and terrified."

"She may be scared, but she's tougher than all of us put together," Aiden insisted. "We did Mac Mulvey stuff all the time when we were fugitives! Dad—you of all people should recognize something from your own book!"

Agent Sorenson appeared in the doorway. "Well, I made some inquiries. It's nothing. Pranks—teenagers with too much time on their hands."

John Falconer let out a long breath. "I guess that's it then."

Aiden was appalled. "That's not 'it'! All he did was talk on his cell phone!"

"I spoke to local law enforcement," Sorenson amended. "You know what they told me? 'It's football season.' Every time there's a big game coming up, the local high school kids suddenly turn into comedians."

"But aren't you even going to assign an agent to go over there to check it out?"

The agent was impatient. "This is a kidnapping investigation. I don't have the kind of manpower where I can send agents chasing after nonsense."

"No," Aiden agreed caustically. "Not when they're so busy standing around doing nothing."

"A waiting game is not 'doing nothing'!" Sorenson snapped.

Louise Falconer took her son's face between her hands. "Calm down, Aiden. It only hurts Meg's chances when we squabble among ourselves."

Aiden played his trump card. "Agent Harris followed up on my hunch before, and it turned out to be right."

Sorenson bristled, and his cheeks flushed.

John Falconer jumped in quickly. "Harris isn't here now, and nobody misses him. He had his chance and he could have gotten your sister killed, and you, too. Can't you see that?"

All Aiden saw was that his parents were so desperate with worry that they could no longer think clearly. Two brilliant criminologists so freaked out that they were powerless to help their own daughter.

Sleep.

Time and time again Meg wrestled it away. But as the Buick continued west on Route 119, her exhaustion outlasted her resolve. She had spent four days living at the limit of tension and endurance. The darkening sky, the numbing vibration of the car — the combination was like knockout drops.

She awoke to find a pillowcase over her head. She struggled, but a strong force — Spidey? — held it in place.

"Easy," soothed Tiger's voice.

She was being carried by her legs and under her arms. The hood was loose around her neck, and she could look down through a narrow opening. Packed dirt and underbrush passed beneath her.

A forest path?

They're going to kill me and bury me in the woods!

But that made no sense. If they really meant to murder her, they could have done it anytime in the past few days. They wanted ransom. She was worthless to them dead.

So why the nature hike? A hideout, maybe?

Meg watched the odd close-up movie that was playing below her. From such a short distance off the ground, it was impossible to make out any landmarks. She tried to get a sense of just how far they had traveled on foot. A mile? A mile and a half? It seemed as if they'd been walking forever. She was pretty sure the trail was becoming steeper.

A mountain?

At last, Mickey's voice asked, "Is this it?"

Meg could see nothing, just rocky ground covered by weeds and underbrush. Then she was tipped up to a better angle and caught a glimpse of a log-frame cottage. Separate from the house itself was a pair of flat, wooden cellar doors. Tiger crouched into Meg's pinched field of vision and pulled open the weathered panels, revealing a cobweb-strewn stairway.

It looked worse than any dungeon, a descent into total darkness.

Pure irrational fear gripped her. "You can't make me go down there!"

Tiger was calm. "We can make you do whatever we want."

Spidey and Mickey swung her into the opening and set her feet down on the top step. It was the first solid ground she'd felt in more than an hour. Her legs were like rubber. They nearly crumpled beneath her as she wheeled around on the stair, tearing off the pillowcase-hood to confront her captors.

"I won't go!"

Spidey grinned at her, almost leering.

He's enjoying this!

He reached out and shoved her. Flailing helplessly, she pitched down the stairs, tumbling into the shadowy cellar. At the bottom, her head smacked against the hard floor, and the blackness was complete.

1-202-555-7487.

The business card was crumpled, but the number was still legible. Not that Aiden could ever forget it.

Emmanuel Harris's cell phone number.

He began to dial, only to put the handset back in its cradle before he was halfway through.

What am I, crazy?

This was J. Edgar Giraffe, the enemy who had hounded Aiden and Meg over seven thousand miles . . .

But, like a heat shimmer on a distant highway, his bathroom vandal theory danced before him. He'd had a way-out hunch like this once before. His own parents hadn't even taken it seriously. It had been Harris who'd grudgingly followed up on it.

He might believe me now . . .

1-202-555-7487.

He almost chickened out again when the phone started ringing.

For Meg, he reminded himself.

At the sound of the hated voice, he blurted, "It's Aiden Falconer—"

"This is Harris. Leave a message." A beep called for his voicemail.

The words came pouring out. "I found Meg—at least I think I did. But Sorenson—the new agent—he won't even listen to me. I know you're off the case, but you've got to help—"

The tone cut him off in midsentence. It was as if the towering agent himself had slammed a door in his face.

What a waste of time! Why would J. Edgar Giraffe care what was going on with Meg? This wasn't his case anymore. For all Aiden knew, he was out of town, maybe even out of the country.

Harris was not the answer. Neither was Sorenson. Or even Mom and Dad.

Nobody was going to help him help Meg.

It was up to Aiden and Aiden alone to follow the trail of vandalized bathrooms to his sister. He was the only one who could do it, because he was the only one who *would* do it.

The question was how.

7

The dark blue Ford Taurus might as well have had UNMARKED POLICE CAR stenciled on its side, FBI Agent Frank Ortiz decided. Surely half the population of Maryland—and a good chunk of Virginia and DC as well—had already spotted him parked at the curb, keeping an eye on the Falconer home.

A tall, thin teen waved as he turned up the front walk. "Hi, Agent Ortiz," the kid said.

Aiden's friend. Richie Somebody. It was impossible to mistake him because he always wore a baseball cap from some minor league team he loved. The kid was never seen without it.

"Perfect timing," Ortiz called. "Your buddy could use a little cheering up. He's kind of depressed today."

"Gotcha." Richie rang the bell and disappeared inside.

Nice guy, Ortiz reflected. Loyal. Loyalty was always in short supply around the Falconers. A lot of people, including even some of Ortiz's colleagues in the FBI, still considered them traitors.

A while later, the baseball cap emerged from the house. The tall gangly teen beneath the low visor waved to him before heading briskly down the street. Ortiz waved back. It was his first action of the past hour aside from watching and waiting.

Had Ortiz looked closer, he might have noticed that the boy wearing Richie's hat and Richie's jacket was not Richie. But the FBI man was guarding against threats from the outside; why would he give a second thought to a close family friend?

Police work seemed exciting on TV, but the day-to-day of it was boring in the extreme.

The Greyhound bus headed west out of downtown Baltimore, wending its way through traffic onto the interstate that would take it to the south and west toward central Virginia.

In the shadow of Richie Pembleton's beloved Greenville Cubs baseball cap, Aiden pored over a sheaf of papers—the article about the bathroom vandals, and online maps of every town, village, burg, and hamlet along a hundred miles of Route 119. They were remarkably few and far between.

They've taken Meg to the moon, or at least halfway.

How was he ever going to find her out here?

He had told no one of his plan to search for his sister

on his own. His parents would have nailed him to his bed to prevent it. They certainly would have asked Sorenson and the FBI to stop him. Even Richie, his accomplice, knew only that Aiden was going, but not where. When Mom and Dad walked in on the boy, curled up under the covers of Aiden's bed, Richie wouldn't have anything to tell them.

It would be a shock for his parents. He felt bad about that. But as long as they continued to rely on do-nothing Sorenson, Aiden had to take matters into his own hands. For Meg, doing nothing amounted to a death sentence.

He peered out the window at the passing countryside. They were moving at a good speed now, but the ride was frustrating. Every time they seemed to be making progress, the bus would pull off the interstate into some one-horse town. It was maddeningly slow, especially since reaching Route 119 wasn't half the battle. Once he got to the area, he didn't know how to track down Meg, or if his theory of her whereabouts was even correct. And if, by some miracle, he really did locate her, he didn't have the first idea how to get her away from three armed-and-dangerous kidnappers. He had already lost a confrontation with one of them, and nearly cost the FBI two million dollars' ransom money in the bargain.

Just thinking of each impossible task ahead gave him a

migraine. Once he stepped off this bus, he had absolutely no transportation. The clues that held the secret of Meg's whereabouts could be anywhere along a hundred-mile stretch of road.

How am I supposed to cover that kind of distance — by jogging?

On top of it all, he was a runaway. When his parents realized he was gone, they'd call in the FBI in a heartbeat. Sorenson would put out another APB on another missing Falconer. People would be looking for him — not a major manhunt like his fugitive days, but he definitely had to keep a low profile.

The bus slowed as it took the jug handle and exited into another community — really just a cluster of houses and a gas station. He groaned as he read the sign in front of the roadside luncheonette that served as the depot:

EAT HERE

GET GAS

If he'd had any sense of humor left, he would have laughed out loud.

The driver pulled up to a scratched Plexiglas bus shelter and opened the doors. Nobody got on or off. It was just another useless stop to turn this simple trip into a hideous all-day marathon.

Then he spotted the name stenciled on the milky Plexiglas: KERWIN.

All at once he was wrestling with fourteen pages of printouts from MapQuest. There he found—the meandering hairline of Route 119, and somewhere along its path . . . the tiny dot of Kerwin, Virginia.

A sharp hiss announced the closing of the doors.

"Hey—hey wait!"

Juggling airborne papers, Aiden sprinted for the exit.

Meg awoke to a cold, damp feeling on the side of her head that hurt like crazy. She cried out in shock and pain. A firm grip on her shoulders contained her struggles.

"Everything's okay," soothed a friendly voice. "It's just me."

"Aiden?" But when her eyes blinked open, the kidnapper she called Mickey came into focus.

"Hold still," he advised, dabbing at her with a wet cloth, stained pink.

She winced from the sting. "What is this place?"

The young man's expression grew wary, and Meg knew he would not tell her. But she remembered the isolated mountain cabin, the open cellar doors leading to darkness.

This must be the basement.

She took in her surroundings. A single flickering candle lit the stone-lined walls, giving the cellar the appearance of an underground tomb. A pile of clay flowerpots, most of them broken, filled one corner. Against the opposite wall leaned an assortment of rusted gardening tools — cultivators, hoes, spades, and rakes.

"Congratulations," she mumbled. "You've found another five-star hotel to put me up in."

"Hang in there," Mickey soothed. "You'll be home soon."

"Or I'll be dead soon," she amended bitterly.

He was genuinely distressed. "Don't talk like that! We're not murderers!"

"Maybe *you're* not. But can you say the same thing about your two friends up there? He's a goon, and she's worse. She talks friendly — until you pay attention to what she says."

"It's not like that. We're just trying to —" He looked guilty. "You know what we're trying to do."

"That's all I am to you — ransom money. Too bad you can't stick me in an ATM and make it spit out cash."

The young man bristled. "It's easy to look down on money when you've always had plenty of it!"

Meg snorted. "Like there's an excuse for kidnapping."

"I'm not making excuses," he retorted. "I'm just telling it like it is. My brother's in trouble. He needs a lawyer — a good one, the kind that doesn't come cheap. I've been looking after the kid since I was sixteen and he was twelve. What am I going to do — work at Burger King? His trial will be ancient history before I can pay for his defense."

Meg swallowed a sarcastic *boo-hoo.* She had no sympathy for criminals. What she did have was a vast understanding of the connection between siblings. Four years. That was the same as her age difference with Aiden. She would never forget their weeks on the run, when they had been each other's only support. To this day, there was nothing Meg would not do for Aiden, and he for her. Kidnapping? It had never come to that. But Meg was almost certain that anything meant *anything.*

"What kind of trouble is your brother in?" she asked finally.

"The worst kind," Mickey admitted. "He got mixed up with a gang. I was working on a fishing boat. Ten-day run. By the time I got back —" He clenched his fists for emphasis. "I have to get him a good lawyer! He's going to college. He's not going to end up like me!"

In spite of herself, Meg was touched by her captor's attempt to save a loved one the horrors of prison. It was all too familiar. And while Mom and Dad had been released in the end, the fate of the Falconer family could hardly be described as happily ever after.

Brought back to her own problems, Meg tuned Mickey out as he went on and on about his hopes for his younger brother. Her eyes fixed on the labors of a small black beetle. It was digging diligently at a crumbling mortar course in the fieldstone wall. She watched, squinting in the dim orange glow, as the little creature managed to burrow itself into a crack and disappear.

Her gaze shifted to the collection of gardening tools. *If that bug can dig out, so can I.*

Agent Emmanuel Harris had known better weeks. His removal from the Falconer kidnapping still stung. He didn't blame his superiors for yanking him — he had bungled the rescue attempt, and put not just Meg, but also Aiden, at risk. Yet he didn't see how Mike Sorenson represented any kind of improvement. Sorenson had a reputation as a by-the-book agent, not a creative thinker. And precious little about the Falconer family ever seemed to go by the book.

It's not your case anymore, he was quick to remind himself.

He'd wanted so much to help those poor people after all the suffering he'd caused them. Instead, he'd failed them again.

Then there was the embarrassing matter of the cell phone. It had slipped out of his shirt pocket as he'd leaned over the coffeepot. The verdict — liquid damage. Beyond repair. Bad enough he'd been pulled from the case. Now he was the laughingstock of the FBI.

He clutched the new replacement phone tightly as he entered the common room where the DC field agents had their offices. Several dozen staffers were on hand to greet him. At the sight of his towering six-foot-seven-inch frame, the crowd raised their coffee mugs in a welcoming toast. A cell phone sat in each and every one. Held high in salute, the handsets all rang at the same moment — a cacophony of electronic tones.

Harris felt heat rushing to his cheeks. "Hilarious," he muttered, and disappeared into his office.

He powered up the new phone. Thirty-six unheard voice messages. Terrific. He wasn't even reassigned and he'd already fallen behind. With a sigh, he pressed the key to play the first one — and heard the words that brought his attention screeching back to the case he was trying to put behind him.

"I found Meg . . ."

Richie Pembleton had made it to Level 9 Jedi Master on Aiden's computer when Louise Falconer came in.

"Aiden, you didn't have any lunch, and—" She blinked. "Oh, hi, Richie. Where's Aiden?"

He had been waiting for that question all day, yet when it finally came, it still caught him off guard. "He—left."

The conversation that followed was every bit as awful as he'd feared it would be. First he faced the disbelief of Aiden's mother. Then came John Falconer's shock and anger. Finally, he was dragged in front of Agent Sorenson of the FBI.

"How dare you interfere with a federal investigation?"

Richie was cowed. "I didn't interfere with anything! I just gave him my hat and my jacket—"

"You deliberately let him impersonate you so he could run away!" the lead agent accused.

"He said it was Meg's only chance!" Richie quavered.

"What else did he say?" Aiden's father cut in. "Where was he going?"

"He didn't tell me! Honest! He just said the FBI wouldn't listen, and he was doing what he had to."

Sorenson was enraged. "Aiden Falconer is a material witness in this case! Helping him flee is a federal crime! I could have you arrested—"

"But you won't," drawled a familiar voice from the doorway.

Stooping slightly to keep from whacking his head on the frame, Agent Harris stepped into the house. "See, if you arrest Richie, that calls attention to the fact that Aiden Falconer walked out of this house right under your nose."

Sorenson turned on him. "You have no business here. You're not on this case anymore."

Harris shrugged. "I'm here as a private citizen, a friend of the family."

John Falconer choked. "You're no friend of ours!"

"Aiden called me," Harris informed them. "He left me a message that said he'd figured out where Meg was. Know anything about that?"

"It was nonsense," snapped Sorenson. "A wild theory about blocked toilets."

"I want every detail," Harris insisted.

Sorenson was appalled. "You're taking this seriously?"

"Aiden takes it seriously," Harris returned. "Crazy or

not, that's the lead he'll be following. It may have escaped you, but we now have *two* missing kids."

Sorenson hung on stubbornly. "Aiden's been gone less than twenty-four hours. He's not a missing person yet."

It was Louise Falconer who relented. "Come with me, Agent Harris. I'll show you the Internet article Aiden found."

The hamburger at EAT HERE, GET GAS was barely edible, but Aiden devoured every crumb. He hadn't known he was hungry; he'd been far too uptight for that. But in his anxiety to sneak out of the house as Richie, he had skipped breakfast, and now it was late afternoon. This overcooked greasy patty on a soggy bun was better than any gourmet meal.

He leaned back on the stool, keeping an eye on the TV screen mounted above the counter. It was tuned to Fox News, and he was grateful to note that he wasn't featured in the broadcast. Maybe his departure hadn't been noticed at home yet. So he could operate freely — whatever that meant. He didn't even have transportation to the rest stops mentioned in the article.

A voice from the other end of the counter reached him. "Archie called in sick again. Guess he doesn't like delivering hay any more than I do."

"He wouldn't work for me," the counterman vowed.

"Haven't got much choice," the farmer complained. "What I can afford to pay, they're not exactly lining up for the job." He slammed down his coffee mug. "I've got four more stops west of here. It'll be a miracle if I get home before midnight!"

Aiden directed his gaze out the window. A tractor was parked there. Attached to it was a long trailer piled high with hay bales.

Transportation.

He paid his bill and left the restaurant. Once outside, he circled back to the hay wagon in the lot. When the two heads in the luncheonette were turned away, he climbed onto the trailer and lay down among the bales.

A few minutes later, the tractor started up, and he was on his way west on Route 119.

The roar of the diesel motor, the bumpy motion, and the sweet smell of new-mown hay reminded him of every hayride at every fall fair he had ever visited. The memory clouded. Meg had usually been beside him, teasing him as the mosquitoes ate him alive and didn't touch her. He would gladly have sacrificed his skin to every bug on the planet to have her with him now.

Those hayrides had been brief. Aiden had never considered the result of the constant jostling motion of the wagon over endless miles. He had to consider it now, because it was making him queasy. It would be hard to stay hidden if he started throwing up.

Just as he was about to succumb to a bout of landlubber's seasickness, he spied a gas station coming up on the right. The sign advertised a mechanic. He pulled the folded papers out of his pocket. The Internet story included an interview with a mechanic—supposedly the only one on this stretch of road. This had to be one of the four places!

Keeping low, he slithered between hay bales until he reached the edge of the flatbed. He paused, watching the pavement rushing by below him. The tractor wasn't as fast as a car, but they had to be doing at least twenty-five or thirty. A guy could get pretty messed up throwing himself off a vehicle moving at that speed.

The garage was directly beside them. The time to jump was *now*! Aiden aimed for some tall grass and hurled himself off the flatbed. He landed face-first on the gravel of the shoulder before rolling down into the softness of the ditch.

He did a brief check of his bones and lay there, relieved, catching his breath.

"Hey, buddy," called a disgusted voice from the tractor. "If you'd asked, I'd have given you a lift."

So much for staying hidden. He had just risked life and limb for nothing.

Stop complaining, he told himself. *You're here. And with any luck, they'll remember Meg.*

"They" turned out to be the mechanic who operated the snack bar, pumped gas, and sold lottery tickets when he wasn't fixing cars. He seemed absolutely astonished when Aiden brought up the subject of the blocked toilet from two days before.

"Who are you? The Undersecretary of Toilets? What do you care about our plumbing problems?"

"I'm not interested in your toilet," Aiden explained patiently. "I just need to know about the people who blocked it."

"They came in with a blowout," the mechanic recalled. "I sold them a new tire, and they left—after using the bathroom, obviously."

"But do you remember what they looked like?" Aiden persisted. "Did they have a young girl with them?"

"Yeah, about ten or eleven," the man nodded. "My money's on her. She and her mom were the only ones who went back there. A grown woman wouldn't jam a whole roll of paper down a toilet. That's some kid's idea of a joke."

"What about their car?" Aiden urged. "Make? Model? Color? License plate?"

The mechanic shrugged. "It might have been green, but don't hold me to that. They seemed to be in a hurry.

Gave me cash. I'm pretty sure they were heading west. I wish I had more for you. I was barely paying attention until Niagara Falls came out the back door."

"Thanks for your help," Aiden said, and meant it sincerely. Just the thought that Meg had actually been here — that the trail wasn't totally cold — made his heart soar.

Where to next? The kidnappers were heading west, but that wasn't exactly an address. Besides, he was stranded here. The farmer with the hay wagon was long gone. What should he do? Hitchhike? It was already getting dark. Who knew when the next car would come by?

The thought had barely crossed his mind when a shiny new pickup truck squealed to a halt alongside the fuel pumps. Two teenagers hopped out. One began to fill the tank; the second ran around the back of the building to the bathroom.

Should I ask for a lift? Aiden wondered. The farmer would have taken him. Maybe these kids would, too.

But his gut instinct was to remain invisible. No one was looking for a runaway yet, but that could change at any minute.

Staying in the shadows of a few scrub bushes, Aiden worked his way around to the back of the vehicle. Perfect. The payload was covered by a tarp.

If I play my cards right, they'll never know I'm back there.

So focused was he on his stealthy approach to the pickup that he completely missed it when something under the tarp moved.

10

Meg jammed the blade of the hoe into the crack where she'd seen the intrepid beetle disappear. The mortar crumbled, raining dust and pebbles down on her. She began to worry the point of the hoe in the opening, digging it deeper into the gap between fieldstones. More debris showered her. Soon she was white with dust. But that was only a fraction as dirty as she hoped to be pretty soon. If she could break through these stones, she could tunnel out of this prison. It would only be a matter of a few feet to the surface.

It had been at least an hour since Spidey had brought her dinner—a stale submarine sandwich in a plastic wrap. She would have loved to throw it at him. But a night of digging required energy. And food equaled fuel.

"When you're ready to sleep, blow out the candle," he'd grunted. She hoped that meant her kidnappers wouldn't check on her again until morning—at which time they would find her long gone.

At last, the hoe was in deep enough for her to finesse

the blade behind the stone. She leaned on the handle, throwing her full eighty pounds into the effort of levering the first piece out of the wall.

The rock wouldn't budge. As she grunted and pushed, sweat began to trickle from her brow, tracking through the dust and dirt on her face. For the first time, she faced the possibility that she might not be strong enough to pull this off. That thought amped up her power level, and she gave a mighty heave. With a snap, the wooden handle broke at the blade, sending Meg sprawling. Enraged, she speared the broken pole into the crack. To her surprise, it stuck there. And when she attempted to free it, she felt the stone move.

Encouraged, she leaned into it. There was a crunching, and the rock came away from the wall. Behind it was hard-packed earth. Few sights had ever looked so beautiful to Meg Falconer.

She grabbed a small spade and began to excavate the opening. The dirt was dense and solid, but still much easier to deal with than stone. In no time, she had hollowed out the beginning of her passage. Now all she had to do was widen the entrance.

She filled the hole with as many gardening tools as she could cram inside. Then she wrapped her arms around the bouquet of wooden handles and pulled with all her might.

The result was astonishing, and not a little scary. The weakened wall disintegrated, crumbling to pieces at her feet. Two more fieldstones came loose and toppled out, missing her toes by inches. The candle flickered dangerously in the flying dust, but did not go out.

A good omen, she decided.

One escape tunnel, coming up.

She began to dig, loosening the soil with the point of the spade. It was a thousand times filthier than she'd expected. Since she was tunneling at a sharp angle up, every shovelful rained straight down onto her head. The effort to keep from coughing and spitting loud enough to alert her captors was almost as difficult as the actual work. Her eyes stung, and she could barely breathe. But she did not slow down.

Soon she was so deep inside that she could no longer work from the floor. She had to hoist herself into the passageway, bracing her feet against the backside of the fieldstone wall. She tried to shovel the mess around her left shoulder and behind her body. She was sure it was piling up in the basement, but that was fine with Meg. She never intended to go back there — not in this life.

Up she burrowed, pushing through the earth like a mole. The darkness was near total. The air was stale, and almost nonexistent. She was aware of a horrid gritty taste in her mouth. She spat. Mud.

Her excitement level kept back the exhaustion. Where was the surface? This was only a basement! She wasn't coming up from China!

She felt a growing dread. She'd once read about scuba divers losing track of which way was up. Could that happen underground? And then she felt her spade break through a hard, crusty surface.

This is it! You're almost out!

She shoveled madly, desperate to experience cool, clean air. Abandoning the spade, she clawed at the ground above her, hoisting herself up. To her dismay, all she encountered was more earth, softer, moister, smellier.

What's going on? Where's the outside? Why does it stink like rotten garbage?

She had held it together until that moment. But when the panic gripped her, it was unreasoning and total. She was suffocating in black filth. She flailed her arms and legs wildly, which only served to stir up the soft marshy stuff that imprisoned her.

Her entire being was awash with horror. Had she escaped from the cellar only to disappear off the face of the earth, buried alive?

The cabin was tiny and badly in need of a paint job. There was only one bedroom, but that was okay. No one was planning to get much sleep here. For Meg's captors, this was a hideout, pure and simple. A place to lie low and regroup after they'd been forced to flee the warehouse in Alexandria.

Spidey walked in the door, puffing and cursing, holding up a copy of *USA Today*. "Two hours to get a lousy paper!" he spat. "Plus, you've still got to climb a mountain after you park the car!"

"When you're holding a front-page hostage, you don't set up shop in Times Square," Tiger explained, not very patiently. She took the newspaper and headed back outside. "Come on. The sooner we can send a new ransom demand, the sooner we can get paid and disappear."

That was the purpose of the newspaper. A photograph of Meg Falconer holding up today's paper showed not only that she was alive and unhurt, but also proved that the picture was up-to-date.

"How much are we asking for now?" asked Mickey.

"Three million," Tiger said grimly. "The extra million is a penalty for double-crossing us last time."

The kidnappers went outside and removed the wooden stake that was wedged under the handles of the cellar doors to prevent Meg from opening them.

"Come on up, Margaret," Spidey ordered. No answer. "I said come up!"

"We're not going to hurt you," Mickey promised. "We just want to take another picture."

Silence.

The three clattered down the stairs. And gawked.

A mountain of earth and stones sat on the basement floor underneath the entrance to Meg's tunnel. Of Meg herself, there was no sign.

Spidey bounded across the floor and virtually flew into the opening. When he came down, he was pulling Meg by one ankle.

She collapsed into the dirt, spitting and gasping. Her face was pale, her lips blue.

Spidey was enraged. "That'll teach you to try running on us! You almost got yourself killed! Stupid kid!"

Almost smothering had only boosted Meg's frustration and bewilderment. "I was out!" she wheezed. "Why wasn't I out?"

Tiger sniffed the rotting scent in the tunnel and went upstairs to check. When she returned, she was smiling with satisfaction. "You dug yourself into the composter. All you had to do was open the lid, and you would have been home free."

Meg was devastated. She had escaped—if only she could have recognized it!

Tiger was relentless. "If you had gotten out and tried to find your way through these woods on your own, you wouldn't have lasted a day. So cheer up, Margaret. That composter just saved your life."

Spidey thrust the copy of *USA Today* into her hands and hefted his camera. "Say cheese."

"Don't be ridiculous!" Tiger snapped. "We have to clean her up first." She grinned. "Her own mother wouldn't recognize her like this." She snatched the paper away.

Meg sat up, peering at the date above the headline. "Wait a minute! Is it really November sixteenth?"

"What do you care?" snarled Spidey. "You're not going anywhere."

"Tomorrow's my birthday," she replied, and burst into tears.

11

It took only a few breathless seconds for Aiden to real-
ize he was not alone under the tarp in the back of the
pickup. Something — something warm — was sniffing
at his face. A tongue tasted the skin of his cheek, and he
jumped back as if he'd been burned.

Then it spoke, identifying itself in a single syllable:
"*Ma-a-a-a!*"

A *goat*?

He lifted a corner of the tarp to let in a little more
light. A groggy-looking billy goat lay on its side just a
few inches away, watching him with little interest. A
royal purple blanket proclaimed it to be "Abe Jr."

What was it doing back there, obviously hidden? And
why was it so sleepy? Was it sick, and they were taking
it to a vet?

Should I get out of here?

Who knew if he'd find another ride? And the animal
seemed docile enough —

The two teenagers made his mind up for him. While

he was trying to decide what to do, they got into the truck's cab and roared off.

The motion of the truck seemed to lull Abe Jr. In truth, Aiden felt pretty lulled himself. It was getting darker by the minute, and he hadn't had a proper night's rest since Meg had been kidnapped nearly a week ago. He kept himself awake by making up excuses and apologies to use on whatever goat doctor might throw back the tarpaulin and find him stowed away there with the patient.

But the next stop was no vet's surgery. It was a small farmhouse. There they picked up another teen.

This one was in a state of high excitement. "Please — tell me you don't have Abe Jr. back there!"

"Chill out," advised the driver. "We gave him half a sleeping pill. He's mellow."

The newcomer was not soothed. "Dude, the coach at Lincoln High went to school and saw the empty cage! They know it's us, man! The whole football team's out looking for us! We've got to find a place to stash the goat before we're caught with it!"

As Aiden listened, it all came clear to him. This wasn't a sick goat; this was a *hot* goat! He remembered the local cops' reply to Agent Sorenson's inquiries about the bathroom vandals — "It's football season."

Isn't it just my luck to end up in the middle of a feud be-
tween rival high schools over a stolen mascot?

His stomach tightened. Being trapped in a pickup with
a goat had its funny side. But what Aiden was trying to
do here was deadly serious. If he was beaten senseless by
an enraged football team out for revenge, where would
that leave his sister? He was the only one looking for her
where she actually was! A trip to the emergency room
could lead to him being identified as a runaway. If he got
shipped home, he'd be leaving Meg high and dry.

"Get in the truck!" the driver ordered.

Their new accomplice scrambled aboard, and the
pickup peeled away. They must have decided on a hiding place for Abe Jr. Wherever it was, they were headed
there at ninety miles an hour.

Aiden held on for dear life as the pitching of the truck
rolled him and Abe Jr. around the payload. He had already decided that the next time they stopped, he was
gone. No way was he going to bet his sister's life on
some silly high school caper. Sure, he'd be seen making
his exit, but that wouldn't matter. These kids were too
engrossed in their own problems to worry about a total
stranger who came from nowhere and then disappeared
into the same place.

They sped around for a while, and Aiden could hear

snippets of urgent shouted cell phone conversations coming from the cab. That, and a juicy munching sound, almost like—

He stared in horror. Somewhere amid the twists and turns, the maps had worked their way out of his pocket, and Abe Jr. was *eating* them!

"Hey—cut it out!" he hissed, snatching the mangled papers from the goat's mouth. Panic rose in Aiden's gorge. A few shreds of moist white pulp were all that remained.

Calm down, he told himself. *You've already come as far as the directions could take you.* From here, finding Meg would depend on his own ingenuity and pure luck.

After a few minutes, the truck left the road and began to jounce across a stubbly field. Aiden risked a peek out of the tarpaulin. He could see two more sets of headlights in the gloom. Obviously, this was the powwow of the conspiracy against Abe Jr. and Lincoln High.

Aiden made his decision then and there. As soon as the meeting started, he would slip away into the darkness. He would find a barn or shed to shelter in for tonight, and resume his search in the morning. The only sure thing was that he had to get away from this craziness before he got caught up in it.

He felt the truck stop, and heard the slamming of

many doors. He thrust aside the tarp and raised himself to a crouch, still under cover of the cab of the truck.

A group of boys, maybe nine or ten of them, were having a frantic conversation in the glow of three sets of headlights.

Aiden experienced a strange moment of jealousy. A bunch of high school kids involved in a wild prank suddenly seemed like the greatest luxury in the world.

I wonder what it feels like to do something for fun, even stupid fun. . . .

The Falconers always seemed to be scratching and clawing for their very lives. Fun never entered the picture anymore.

Breathing a whispered "Good luck" to Abe Jr., who was beginning to doze, Aiden dropped to the ground and began to steal away across the field.

All at once, there was a loud *bloop* and searchlights blazed in the darkness. Before Aiden had a chance to run, a police car was herding him into a circle with the other boys.

A booted sheriff in a cowboy hat stepped forward, his face grim.

"All right, fellas. Cough up the goat."

12

Sheriff Atkin of Alberta County, Virginia, was doing his best to intimidate the goat-nappers into believing they were in real trouble with the law. That was the only way to deal with these high school mischief-makers — to scare them straight. A long uncomfortable night in lockup was enough for most teenagers. They were so terrified of facing their angry parents the next morning that the vast majority left the building law-abiding citizens.

He was having trouble, though, with that one lanky kid with the strange baseball cap. He refused to give even his name.

"Come on, son. I'll find out sooner or later. Who are you?"

The boy was a clam.

The sheriff turned to the others. "Anyone care to supply the name of this fine, upstanding young man?"

The clam's partners in crime jammed their hands into their pockets, and hemmed and hawed.

Teenagers! Atkin thought in disgust. *They'd rather cut off their tongues than rat one another out.*

The silent boy was carrying no wallet, but he had sixty-eight dollars in cash and a Baltimore County Public Library card in his jacket pocket that identified him as Richard Pembleton.

"City boy, huh? What are you doing out here, Richard? Visiting? Who and where?"

No reply.

The sheriff heaved a sigh. "You'll all be enjoying the hospitality of the county while I get in touch with your parents." He turned to Richard Pembleton. "And when I find yours, I'm going to make a special point of telling them how pleasant and cooperative you've been."

The Alberta County sheriff's office was a long double-wide trailer, set up on concrete blocks. It was in the whistle-stop town of Keyes, the county seat. There was no holding cell large enough for ten people, so Aiden and the other teens were locked in the staff lounge, a small coffee room with a couch, table, chairs, and an adjoining bathroom.

The questions started almost immediately after the door closed.

"How did *you* get here?" demanded Matt, the driver of the pickup. "Who *are* you?"

Aiden could still find no words. What the sheriff had taken for stubbornness was actually his pure horror at what had happened to him. Against all odds, he had picked up Meg's trail, only to get arrested for something he hadn't done! Yet he couldn't even claim his innocence, because that would only point out the fact that he didn't belong. That was far worse than being part of a conspiracy to steal a mascot. Atkin was treating this more as a prank than a crime. But when the sheriff found out his mystery prisoner was a runaway, not a visitor, he'd start to get serious. He might contact the Pembletons of Baltimore County and find out exactly who had Richie's library card. Sooner or later, the FBI would get wind of it. Then Agent Sorenson would send someone to drag him home in disgrace. And where would that leave Meg?

"Listen," he said finally, "I've got no beef with any of you guys."

Jason, who had first sounded the warning that Abe Jr.'s disappearance had been discovered, spoke up. "Are you new around here? You don't go to our school. Are you a spy from Lincoln?"

Matt had to laugh. "Yeah, right. With a forged library card." He faced Aiden. "My question is what were you doing in that field with us? And why did you let Atkin arrest you for something you had nothing to do with? What are you hiding?"

"Whoa!" The shocked exclamation came from a short, stocky boy whose name was Randy. "That's why you look familiar! You're that kid whose sister got kidnapped! Your parents used to be in jail, right? Falconer! You're Aiden Falconer!"

"Don't be stupid!" Jason scoffed. "The guy's name is Richard Somebody."

"No, it's not!" Randy insisted. "I saw his picture in the paper a million times! He and his sister had the cops running around in circles for two months! They proved their parents were innocent!" He rounded on Aiden. "What are you doing here, man?"

Aiden was halfway through a stammered denial when he noticed that all eyes were on him now. He couldn't be sure if the others recognized him, too, but it was clear that Randy's words made sense to them.

He had been identified.

13

Aiden thought fast. He could still refuse to admit it, but what would be the point? No, it was time to do something that he and Meg had never tried in all their weeks on the run. It was time to trust someone.

"Please—don't turn me in. I'm trying to rescue my sister."

"What—*here?*"

"I think they've taken her somewhere along Route 119. That's why I stowed away in your truck—for a lift. I know I can find her, but I've got to get out of here first."

They all looked bewildered. "How?" came from half a dozen throats.

"We're in the police station," added Matt. "Under arrest."

Aiden realized that, although he was younger than these boys, he was the one with the life experience. As a fugitive, he had learned that no locked door was stronger than the need to get past it.

"There must be some way out of here," he mused.

"A window? A heating vent? A skylight? Through the basement, maybe?"

Randy looked surprised. "There's no basement. This whole cop shop is a double trailer up on blocks."

"A trailer?" The word triggered the memory of *Death in Dixie*, one of his father's detective novels. It featured Mac Mulvey's most ingenious escape. The hero was trapped inside a burning trailer, with the windows boarded up and the doors nailed shut. There was absolutely no way out. But with the walls on fire and the interior filling with smoke, the resourceful Mulvey found one.

"The bathroom!" Aiden exclaimed, and rushed to it, dropping to his knees at the base of the toilet.

"What are you going to do?" wisecracked someone. "Flush yourself out?"

Aiden removed the plastic knobs covering the bolts that held the toilet to the floor. "A trailer has to connect to water and drains," he narrated absently. "That means it has trapdoors for the pipe hookups. I just need the toilet taken off."

The teens were bug-eyed.

"Is that how you made monkeys out of the FBI for all that time?" Matt asked. "By doing stuff like this?"

"We did whatever it took to survive," Aiden grunted,

struggling to loosen the bolts with his bare hands. "Just like I'm doing now."

"You're never going to budge that without a wrench," Jason observed.

They searched every drawer, every cupboard, and every surface in the small kitchen. The closest thing to a tool that they found was a bent coffee spoon.

Aiden pointed to a strange device sitting on the microwave. It looked almost like a bowlegged pair of scissors with grooved rubber where the blades should be. "What's that?"

Matt picked it up and demonstrated. "It's a Jar-meister. Lots of people have them around here because everybody makes their own preserves. See? It fits all sizes of jars, and you can open them even when the lids are stuck."

Aiden took the Jar-meister and shrank the ring down to the smallest size. He fitted it over the first bolt and gave a strong twist. The nut held firm for a moment, and then began to turn. The second bolt was tighter, but even it was no match for the Jar-meister.

Randy and Matt stepped forward and lifted the toilet straight up off the floor and out of the bathroom. Now they could see a large square opening surrounding the drainpipe.

Wasting no time, Aiden stepped down into the hole and stood on the ground below the trailer. It would be a tight squeeze to cram his upper body around the drain and under the floor, but he could make it.

Standing there, visible only from the hips up, he addressed the nine boys he was leaving behind. "Anybody coming with me?"

"What's the point?" sighed Matt, who looked like he was dying to try it. "Our parents already know we're here. Besides—Sheriff Atkin and my dad are second cousins."

Randy stepped forward. "Never mind us. Is there anything we can do to help you?"

"Don't tell the sheriff who I am," Aiden said readily. "Put the toilet back and don't show him how I got out. Let him think he's chasing a ghost."

There were more than a few smiles.

"Good luck, man," said Jason. "I hope you find your sister."

His back scraped painfully against the edge of the opening as Aiden made himself thin and managed to slither under the floor. It was cold on the ground, and damp and rocky. He rolled onto his belly and crawled forward, his face brushing through ancient cobwebs, thick as drapery. There was garbage under there, too, including broken glass and pulpy newsprint.

Up above, the toilet was pushed back over the opening, shutting out what little light was coming down to him.

In the total darkness, a pair of yellow feral eyes burned. Aiden nearly jumped out of his skin, and wriggled faster and harder in the opposite direction. The eyes backed off and disappeared.

When he broke out of the shadow of the trailer into open air, it didn't become a whole lot brighter. Keyes may have been the county seat, but he saw no more than a few dozen lights at this hour, most of them far away and up into the hills. He got to his feet, but stayed low until he had put some distance between himself and the police station.

A horrible thought occurred to him: *I just escaped from the police. I'm a fugitive again.* Worse, Sheriff Atkin had his sixty-eight dollars—not to mention Richie's jacket and his precious Greenville Cubs baseball hat.

If I can't get that back, I'd better not try to show my face around home again!

It was a light thought, but he realized how very much it applied to him. If he couldn't find Meg, a return home would mean nothing.

Without his sister, home wouldn't be home anymore.

14

At the Falconer home, November 17th, Meg's twelfth birthday, was impossibly sad. There had been no word of her since the failed rescue. And now even Aiden was gone.

John and Louise Falconer were at their wits' end. They had not believed anything could be worse than serving prison time. But this tragedy that had befallen their children outstripped everything. And the two of them — brilliant, talented, educated — were powerless to change their family's fate.

They had decided to stand aside and let Sorenson handle the case. Now they weren't sure that had been the right decision. The man was so obsessed with rules and regulations that he was incapable of real police work. He refused to send one of his agents to search for Aiden. Going by the book, he was heading up the Margaret Falconer case, not the Aiden Falconer case. It had been Harris, the family's enemy, who had gone after their son.

So who should they trust? Who should they rely on? Who should they put their faith in?

A Toyota Prius screeched up to the curb in front of

the Falconer house. Rufus Sehorn, the Blog Hog, was so excited that he practically flew up the front walk, waving his laptop like a flag.

Louise Falconer ran out to meet him. "Rufus, please tell me you've got something!"

"A new picture!" Sehorn confirmed breathlessly. "She's alive!"

Within minutes, the Falconers, Sehorn, and Agent Sorenson were gathered around the computer, examining the e-mail that had come to www.bloghog.usa.

There was Meg, her hair matted, her face streaked and dirty, holding up a copy of yesterday's *USA Today*.

"My poor little girl, what have they done to you?" Louise breathed, heartbroken.

Sehorn put an arm around her shoulder. "I felt that way, too, at first. But it's just grooming. She isn't bruised or cut; she hasn't lost weight; she's being treated well enough. She's okay."

"Okay!" groaned Meg's father. "She won't be okay until we get her back!"

The message was right underneath the photo:

THE PRICE IS NOW $3 MILLION
THIS IS YOUR LAST CHANCE
HAVE THE MONEY READY
YOU WILL BE CONTACTED

"Our tech people will trace the e-mail," said Agent Sorenson briskly.

John Falconer sighed. "I think you'll find the message bounced all over the world before it came to Rufus. At least, that's how it was last time."

"One of them must be a hacker," Sorenson concluded, "or they're working with one."

"It sounds like they're giving us time to get the money together," Louise observed, trying to be detached and professional. "The extra million won't be a problem, will it?"

Sorenson looked haughty. "It is the policy of the U.S. government never to negotiate with or pay ransom to kidnappers."

Sehorn was confused. "Nobody's suggesting the money should actually be paid — just used to bait a trap."

"That was Harris's strategy," said Sorenson with stinging sarcasm. "And you see how well it worked out."

"Wait a minute," said John Falconer. "You mean we're not even going to *pretend* to cooperate with them?"

"Absolutely not," Sorenson confirmed.

"But" — Louise was horrified — "that's the only way to draw them out of hiding, and maybe Meg with them! Otherwise we're just sitting around hoping they'll get tired of waiting, and let her go!"

Agent Sorenson did not even bother to contradict her.

The Falconers exchanged a look of sheer despair. In that instant, they understood the desperation that had led their son to abandon the safety and comfort of home to pursue shadows.

Sometimes even a wild-goose chase made more sense than doing nothing at all.

15

The ropes hurt—that's how tight they were. But Meg's kidnappers had decided she could not be trusted to be loose in the house. So she sat stiffly upright in a wooden chair, wrists bound behind her, ankles tied to the legs of her seat. It added a whole new dimension to her captivity. If a gaping portal to another universe opened three inches in front of her, she would be powerless to take advantage of it. She could barely move a muscle.

You're twelve today, she reminded herself. *How do you like it so far?*

Not much at all, actually. Before, there had always been an escape to plan, a next move to contemplate. Now she was reduced to waiting and praying.

Her current cell was the tiny bedroom at the back of the cabin. It was probably a cinch to escape from here—if a person could move. As things were, it may as well have been Devil's Island.

She heard the lock release, and the door swung open. There stood Mickey with a paper sack in his hand. He was beaming from ear to ear.

"I'm glad one of us is having a good day," Meg said sourly.

Undaunted, he tore open the bag to reveal a large chocolate cupcake. Then he struck a long, wooden kitchen match and planted it in the center of the icing. He picked it up and held it in front of her face.

"Make a wish."

Meg could have cheerfully bitten his hand off. "You know what I wish for."

"Well, besides that."

She choked back her anger. Unbelievable! This idiot honestly thought he could make things better — that he could make amends for what he had helped do to her, with a birthday cupcake!

Then — she would have done almost anything to prevent it — this kidnapper, this *criminal*, began humming "Happy Birthday."

"Come on," she mumbled uncomfortably. "Cut it out."

He just kept on humming, grinning his goofy grin. And Meg was his captive audience.

At last, the song was over. "Blow," he invited her.

"No."

"Come on, blow out the candle."

"It's not a candle," she seethed, "and this isn't a party!"

He looked so crestfallen, so disappointed, that the atom

of humor in this awful situation found her funny bone.

"Fine," she said, and blew out the match. "I wished for a pony."

He gazed at her earnestly. "I hope you get one some-day."

She scorched him with a burning look. "Don't go serious on me. Let's enjoy our cake." She watched him break the treat in two. "How am I supposed to eat it? Out of a dog dish?"

In answer, he untied her arms. The comfort of having her hands free was so exhilarating that this really was beginning to feel like a party. And the stale hockey puck of a cupcake tasted like heaven. There was something about chocolate icing—especially that big dollop of it on the end of Mickey's nose—

She was pointing at it and laughing when the door was flung open, and Spidey stormed in.

"What's going on here? Why is she untied?"

"Have a heart," Mickey pleaded. "It's her birthday."

"What's the matter with you?" Spidey roared. "Haven't you seen enough examples of what a little Houdini she is? When I say she has to be tied up, that means all the time—including birthdays, Christmas, and the Fourth of July!"

"It's just her hands," Mickey protested.

"Her *hands*? She can use her hands to untie the rest of

her, you nitwit! Where did we find you—on the bus out of Stupid-town? Do you think we *planned* to end up in some mountain rat-hole? She should be long gone, and we should be counting our money! The last thing we need is another mess-up from the likes of *you*!"

"Hey," Meg said, bristling, "he was just trying to be nice—something you'd know nothing about!"

She and Mickey were both unprepared for the violence of Spidey's response. The big man wheeled and struck Meg with an openhanded slap to the face. The force knocked the chair over, and Meg with it. It was so sudden, and so devastating, that she felt she'd been struck by lightning.

Enraged, Mickey lunged at the older, much larger man, but Spidey warded him off with a contemptuous shove.

"I have to keep *her* alive for the money," he warned. "I'm not getting any money for *you*!"

He yanked Meg's chair back upright and retied her hands so tightly that her fingertips began to tingle. She uttered not one word of complaint. She had been manhandled before, but that was different from being deliberately hit.

For the first time since her abduction, Meg Falconer wanted something just as much as her freedom:

Revenge.

16

Aiden was aware of a low warbling sound — not loud, but all-pervading. His insides vibrated along with it — it seemed to be everywhere, coming from a hundred separate, yet connected, sources.

And then a rooster crowed so close to him that he sat bolt upright and banged his head on a wooden shelf directly above him. He came awake with a painful start, and looked around. Countless pairs of beady eyes were fixed on him. The warbling grew louder, like he was being discussed.

"Chickens!" he exclaimed aloud, and nearly choked on a mouthful of feathers. He was in a henhouse!

It all came back to him — the escape from the police station. He had blundered around in the pitch-dark, battered down by exhaustion, knowing he had to rest before he could go on. He had eventually crawled inside what he'd thought to be a small toolshed.

It was a chicken coop. Filthy, smelly, probably flea-infested. The wave of nausea that rolled over him was so strong that he nearly deposited his hamburger from EAT HERE, GET GAS on the straw-covered floor.

On all fours, he crawled to the door and peered outside. It was barely past dawn—the sun was still low in the sky. The chicken enclosure was deserted, but not far away, over a mesh fence, a farmer was pitching hay with a four-pronged fork.

How would he respond to a stranger running out of his henhouse? Aiden didn't want to find out.

You're okay as long as you stay put, he reminded himself.

That thought had barely crossed his mind when the man set down the pitchfork and hefted a huge bucket brimming with grain.

Grain . . . chicken feed!

Sure enough, he was heading this way. Aiden's heart sank when he saw the empty wire basket in his free hand. Aiden knew exactly what that was for. The grain would draw the chickens out into the yard, allowing the farmer to enter the henhouse to collect eggs. Only, the man was going to find a lot more than a few dozen omelets in training this morning. He was about to walk in on an escapee from the sheriff's lockup, covered in dirt and feathers.

The farmer dumped half of the grain into a bird feeder and began tossing handfuls of the rest around the pen.

At the sound, the entire population of the coop began a scrambling, flapping, clucking stampede for the exit. Aiden pressed himself against the wall in an attempt to steer clear of pecking beaks, flailing wings, and scratching talons. It wasn't pleasant, but he wished it would go on forever.

The farmer approached the henhouse.

Should I run?

Meg would probably try to talk her way out of it. But what reasonable excuse could there be? *Hi, there. I'm doing a school project on poultry . . .*

He could see denim-clad legs right outside the door. Another few seconds—

"George!" called a woman's voice from the distance. "Don't forget to swing by the sheriff's and pick up Matt!"

The legs froze. "Kids these days," harrumphed the farmer. "Stealing a mascot—my old man would have horsewhipped me." He started in the opposite direction.

Breathless, Aiden peered through the opening and watched him disappear behind the barn.

Sometimes it's more important to be lucky than smart.

He fled from the henhouse, hurdled the fence, and dived down into the cover of tall grass. The farm was at the edge of some foothills, with houses sprinkled along the mountainside and sprawling agricultural land below.

There was no town exactly, but he noticed a small strip of buildings along a road halfway up the slope.

That has to be the hub of things around here.

If Meg's trail was still warm, he would find it there.

When Sheriff Atkin stepped into the locked staff lounge, he found more or less what he expected—dark circles under red eyes, a collection of youths who had slept little and worried much. Fear of trouble, he reflected with satisfaction, was often more effective than the real thing.

He found one thing he did *not* expect, however—a group of nine boys, not ten.

He scanned the faces. "Where's Pembleton?"

Blank stares greeted this question. Matt spoke up at last. "It's just us in here, Sheriff. Nobody else."

"Yes, there is—there *was*! Richard Pembleton, the skinny kid from out of town!"

"Uh—sir?" put in Jason. "No disrespect, but what would an outsider want with Abe Jr.? We were just trying to keep him away from the Lincoln game this weekend."

"Don't play me!" the sheriff sputtered. "I have his jacket! His hat! His library card!"

His complexion darkening from pink to red to purple, Atkin searched the staff kitchen. The bathroom was empty. The permanent windows were undamaged. The lock on the door showed no signs of tampering.

The more frustrated he became, the louder he yelled at his nine young prisoners. "You think this is a game? The only law against stealing livestock in this county was passed in 1844 to prosecute *cattle rustlers*! How'd you like to be charged with that?"

They would not break. For whatever reason, they had thrown their loyalty behind Richard Pembleton. How typical for a bunch of teenagers to choose a no-respect juvenile delinquent to idolize.

He'd checked last night to make sure there was no runaway teen named Pembleton, but his investigation had gone no further. Who was this mystery kid, and how had he escaped from a locked room?

"This isn't over," the sheriff promised the nine, and shut them back inside. "Janine!" he barked to his secretary. "Call in the deputies — pronto!"

Janine was surprised. The officers of the Alberta County force were spread out over three shifts. The last time all six had been on duty together was when the entire town of Keyes had to be evacuated due to mudslides on the mountain. "What's going on?" she asked.

"We're going to find Richard Pembleton."

17

The image played itself over and over in Mickey's head: Spidey's open hand making contact with Meg's cheek, the impact upending her chair.

Mickey knew his outrage was silly. They had all committed far more serious crimes than a slap in the face — kidnapping, forced confinement, extortion.

Yet those actions were for *money*. He had a reason for needing money. He was doing a bad thing for a good cause — to help his brother. He assumed the others had their reasons as well. But the slap — violence for the sake of violence, intended purely to hurt —

Get real! he scolded himself. *They're kidnappers! What did you expect them to be like — librarians?*

Here he was, deeply embroiled in a major felony, and he was less than clueless about his two accomplices. Spidey had recruited him for this job, but there was barely a hair of a link between them — a guy who knows a guy who knows a guy.

"I hear you're looking to make some fast money," the burly man had said. He'd called himself Joe, quickly adding that it was not his real name. Nor was Tiger's name actually Marcelle. No connection between her and Spidey. They were never to meet again after the ransom had been paid and the operation was over. No, never, *nada*. The entire partnership was built on fairy dust.

It had seemed sensible back then. One could not betray the others to the police. But suddenly — with the deed half done, and all of them on the hook for a lot of prison time if they were caught — it wasn't enough anymore.

Who are these people I've gotten mixed up with?

His eyes fell on Spidey's laptop computer on the kitchen table. They had started calling it "the paperweight," because, in a cabin with no Internet or electricity, it was about as useful as one. They had to drive to a ski lodge thirty miles away to send messages through Tiger's secure e-mailer.

He was alone with Meg. Spidey and Tiger were out purchasing supplies to tide them over while they thought of a plan for the ransom drop-off. That meant more time freezing in this prehistoric cabin, where they didn't even dare turn on the generator for fear of attracting attention.

He pressed the button, and the machine booted up on battery power. He was looking for a personal journal or diary, but the only document in word processing was a half-finished letter disputing a parking ticket. Opening the browser brought up an error message — no Internet connection. So he clicked on HISTORY and examined the Web pages most recently viewed.

There were a few online maps and some information about this area, and — what was this?

> We're talking about the traitors who sold out their country to terrorists! Everybody knows that the so-called evidence to prove their "innocence" was faked. I agree with the bleeding hearts that they shouldn't be in prison; John and Louise Falconer should have been EXECUTED long ago . . .

John and Louise Falconer? Why was Spidey reading online articles about Meg's *parents*? Was this research to help with the ransom operation?

He sifted through the other postings: A FAMILY OF TREASONOUS SCUM, TERROR'S HELPERS, LETHAL INJECTION FOR THE FALCONERS. It was all extreme stuff, violently anti-Falconer. This was a website for people who refused to believe that Meg's parents were innocent.

Spidey was a Falconer-hater!

The whole kidnapping scheme — the goal wasn't ransom! It was payback against the Falconer family.

And I'm caught in the middle of it.

The cold that gripped him had little to do with the

unheated cabin. What would be the ultimate penalty for Doctors John and Louise Falconer to pay for their treason?

The death of their daughter.

Meg wasn't going to be released, whether her parents paid the ransom or not.

It hit Mickey like a cherry bomb going off between his temples. He wasn't a kidnapper. The plot he'd signed on to amounted to *murder.*

The sound of the front door shocked him out of his reverie. The others! He quickly powered down the computer. Oh, how he wished he could do the same for his racing mind.

He was only trying to help his brother. He had nothing against Meg's parents. He had *less* than nothing against Meg. In fact, he had genuinely come to like her in the past days, and admire her spirit.

I'm no murderer.

What was he going to do?

1ε

Route 119 was so small and insignificant that Harris drove past it three times. At last, he found the weathered sign and made the turn down the rural highway that sliced Virginia in two as it meandered west to the mountains.

About an hour later, he stood on the cracked pavement of a gas station, holding up a photograph of Aiden Falconer.

"Sure, I've seen him," the mechanic said immediately. "He was just here yesterday. We had some plumbing troubles, and he was asking for details."

"I heard about that," the agent told him. "Blocked toilet, right?"

The man rolled his eyes. "Why is the whole world obsessed with my bathroom? It was just some rotten kid's idea of a joke."

Harris showed the man another picture, this one of Meg. "Is this the rotten kid in question?"

"Could be. It's hard to tell. She was wearing a hat and sunglasses. Are you some kind of cop?"

Harris flashed his badge. "FBI."

"FBI?" The mechanic goggled. "It was only a clogged pipe! I fixed it myself, no big deal!"

"The girl was kidnapped six days ago. The boy is her brother. He ran away to look for her on his own. How was he traveling? Did somebody give him a lift?"

"Didn't see him arrive," the man said. "Come to think of it, I don't recall him leaving, either. He was just here, and then he was gone. Sorry."

Harris had no trouble believing that Aiden had appeared from nowhere and disappeared just as quickly. It was exactly the kind of resourcefulness that had made the Falconer kids so hard to catch in their fugitive days. "One more thing—any idea where he was going?"

"West," the mechanic replied. "That's the way his sister was heading, if that's who it was. I told him to look for a green car—hope I was right about that."

"Thanks." Back at his Chevy Trailblazer, Harris dialed his assistant in Washington. "I don't suppose a kid named Aiden Falconer has been picked up along Route 119 in Virginia."

"I'm monitoring all the reports," his assistant confirmed. "No luck so far."

"Do another search," the agent instructed. "Anything involving teenagers in this part of the state." He paused, listening to the hurried typing through the phone.

"One hit—Keyes, Virginia. On my map, it looks

about an hour west of you. A teenage boy escaped sheriff's custody last night. They can't even explain how he got out of the trailer."

Harris felt his pulse quicken. This disappearing act had Falconer written all over it.

"Wait—" His assistant sounded disappointed. "No, dead end. Local high school rivalry, stolen mascot, wrong kid."

"What's the name?" Harris persisted.

"Richard Pembleton."

Sometimes—even without Starbucks—it was worth getting up in the morning.

Richie Pembleton, Aiden's best friend.

"Get that sheriff on the phone."

Quit.

There was no such word in Meg Falconer's vocabulary. No such impulse in her brain. And yet—

Tied stiffly—painfully—to the chair, staring bleakly at the plank walls, it was impossible not to reach one conclusion:

This isn't going well.

All her escape attempts had failed miserably. Worse, her antics had only served to turn her captors into dedicated jailers. This—she struggled vainly against the bonds—was something she had brought on herself.

She wasn't a quitter. But she didn't lie to herself, either.

So if escape wasn't a possibility, what was? Rescue? For all she knew, they were searching for her in Baltimore or DC, hundreds of miles away. No one would ever find her out here in the middle of nowhere. Ransom? Surely that would have happened days ago, if it was going to happen at all. Mom and Dad just didn't have the money.

I'm in big trouble.

A vague thought fluttered around her mind — that Aiden might try to come after her. But heroics like that were part of their fugitive days. And they were not fugitives any longer.

She tried to stay positive, but it was growing harder to do with each passing hour. The truth was she had been in some pretty tough spots, but this was the great-grandmother of all of them. It would take a miracle for her to get out of this alive.

She peered up from her melancholy reverie to see Mickey framed in the doorway, watching her.

"Don't look so sad," he told her.

She glared at him scornfully. Her life was over. What did he expect her to do — dance with joy?

But she couldn't help noticing that he seemed odd, even for him. On edge, indecisive, close to tears.

He stepped in front of her and held out a small silver object. She stared. A nail file? Was he here to give her a manicure? Like the kidnappers were afraid she might claw her way out with long fingernails?

Then he moved behind her, and she felt the file being placed firmly in her right hand.

Shocked, she twisted her head to gawk at him.

"Maybe you had it from the very beginning," he mumbled awkwardly. "It was in your pocket, and we missed it when we searched you."

Meg was thunderstruck. Didn't he know that she would use this file to cut through the ropes that bound her wrists and free herself?

The expression on his face gave her the answer: He *did* know.

He wanted her to escape.

She almost said thank you, but held herself back for fear he might change his mind. Besides, if Spidey and Tiger had any inkling that he had helped her, he would be in danger.

He paused at the door and turned back to her. "I'm sorry," he said quietly. And before she could answer, he was gone.

By the time the door clicked shut behind him, she was already hard at work, sawing at the ropes.

19

The farmhouse looked deserted, and no car stood in the driveway. By now, Aiden had lost track of how many properties he had crossed—six? Seven? He stayed clear of the road, keeping low in the tallest grass. The mountainside seemed no closer, yet he'd been on the move for more than an hour. That meant the hills were farther away than they looked.

He had spotted one police car on a side lane, but the siren had not been on. It had disappeared and not returned.

Maybe they sleep late at the sheriff's office.

Or maybe they just didn't care that much about Richard Pembleton from Baltimore County, who got mixed up in a high school prank.

As soon as he saw the bike leaning against the porch rail, he knew he was going to take it. On foot, he simply couldn't get around fast enough. It might be all day before he reached the mountain. Who knew how much time Meg had left?

The bike was a Trek—new and expensive-looking.

He almost wished it was old and beat-up. The owner wasn't going to be happy about losing it. With any luck, he could leave it in a place where it could be found and returned.

He hopped on and headed for the main road, shifting into a comfortable gear. It was risky to show himself to any passing car. But the way these tires hummed along the asphalt made the risk worthwhile. At least now he was getting somewhere.

He pedaled for the mountains. As the sun rose higher in the sky, the terrain took an upward slant. He down-shifted into lower gear and began to labor up the grade. Soon he was bathed in sweat, despite the cool November air. Last night in the henhouse, he'd thought he would freeze to death.

Exhaustion soon morphed into pain. His legs burned; his chest ached from the lung-lancing effort. Even his eyes stung as perspiration poured down his forehead.

By the time I reach town, I'll be too weak to ask about Meg!

It was nearly noon when he reached the strip of build-ings he had seen from the farm where he'd spent the night. It was a much smaller town than he'd expected —a gas station, a general store, a diner, and a couple of ski shops.

All at once, he felt terribly exposed on his stolen bike. In a place this size, a thousand-dollar Trek might be known to the locals. He hopped off and stashed his ride in an alley between two clapboard structures. When he stepped out, he caught sight of himself reflected in the window of Ski Togs. He looked like exactly what he was—someone who had broken out of custody, spent the night in a chicken coop, and ridden a million miles uphill. If he approached anyone in his present condition, they'd be dialing 911 before he got the first word out. His next stop had to be the gas station bathroom, to get himself cleaned up.

A thought occurred to him—could this toilet have been one of Meg's targets? It scarcely mattered anymore. He knew the kidnappers had been headed this way. It was time to zero in on *them*.

Leaving a lot of feathers and dust and sweat behind, he emerged and went to see the attendant. He found the man on his hands and knees behind the cash register, scrubbing the linoleum floor.

"Hi, I'm looking for some cousins of mine. I think they passed through a couple of days ago. Maybe they stopped here." There was no reply, so Aiden soldiered on. "There were two men and a woman, plus a young girl of eleven—no, twelve—"

My God, he thought to himself. *She's twelve now. She spent her birthday kidnapped.*

"Don't remember people," came the voice from the floor. "Just cars."

"The car," Aiden repeated. "Uh — green. Yes, definitely green."

"Green what?"

"I don't know," Aiden admitted. "Just a regular car, I guess. I'm not sure of the make and model — "

"Doesn't matter," the voice interrupted. "Haven't seen anything green in a while. Kind of early in the season for much traffic."

"Season?"

The man looked up at him. "Ski season. All it takes is a few inches of snow, and this town's jumping."

Aiden couldn't imagine this town jumping even in an earthquake. But he thanked the attendant and stepped back out to the street.

Where to now? He doubted Meg's kidnappers had visited one of the ski shops. His eyes fell on the general store. If they were holed up somewhere around here, surely they'd need supplies.

He got to the shop just as an apron-clad woman backed onto the porch, pulling a wagonload of Ice Melt. Aiden jumped forward and held the door for her.

"Thanks." She began stacking the bags under the window for an outside display, and paused to smile at him. "Something I can do for you?"

Aiden repeated the story about the "cousins" he was looking for. "In a green car," he finished.

She brightened. "You know what? I think I know who you're talking about. A big guy, right?"

Aiden's heart leaped as he thought back to the burly kidnapper in the Spider-Man mask. "He's my—uncle! You've seen him?"

"Just this morning," was the reply. "Not two hours ago. He was with your aunt. They were laying in some groceries. Fixing to stay awhile, I guess."

"Where?" Aiden barely whispered. "I mean, stay where?"

She seemed surprised. "Don't *you* know? They're *your* relatives."

"I—I lost their address—that is—my mom did." He clamped his jaw shut. The storekeeper was beginning to regard him with suspicion.

"Do you live around here? What's your name?"

"I'm—uh—I'm—" Oh, man, he was messing this up! After all his experience as a fugitive, he should have been better at thinking on his feet. But the shock of scoring a direct hit on Meg's kidnappers halfway up Nowhere

Mountain had left him defenseless and stammering. Part of him was celebrating. He had found her—or at least, picked up her trail. Yet, at the same time, he was blowing it with the one person who might be able to help him.

With a sinking heart, he realized that all his attempts to appear friendly and normal were only making things worse.

"I—I gotta go!"

He turned and ran back to the alleyway where he had stashed the bike. Stupid, stupid, stupid to talk to people without having his story straight in his own head.

He wheeled out onto the main drag, tossing the woman what he hoped was a casual wave. Maybe she would consider him just an oddball, because if she called the cops—

No sooner had the thought crossed his mind than the squad car appeared, far too soon for her to have sounded the alarm. It was pure coincidence—bad luck. But it was too late to flee. The cruiser was coming right toward him. His only chance was to brazen it through, ride on, act like he belonged.

He could see the young deputy's eyes now, giving him the once-over, taking note of the expensive Trek. And then—just like that—it was all over. The car drove on; the moment passed.

Aiden let out a long tremulous breath. He was safe.

While he was silently congratulating himself, he heard a fateful noise. The squad car braked, reversed, and backed up alongside him. The window rolled down, and the officer stuck his head out.

"Richard Pembleton?"

Caught!

20

Aiden blasted away from the cruiser, fear driving his pedaling legs. Behind him, the car swung around into a three-point turn.

It was a small head start, not nearly enough for Aiden to outrun a motor vehicle. His only hope was to take the bike where the cruiser couldn't go. He steered around the second ski shop and took off along a dirt path behind the buildings. He could see the deputy paralleling him along the road.

How am I going to get away?

His eyes fell on the sign:

BLUE VALLEY SKI RESORT — GUESTS ONLY

He shot down the gravel lane, which traveled across a high ridge. The ski lodge was visible through the trees far below. And, beyond that, the farms to the east.

Behind him came the sound he'd been dreading — automobile tires crunching on the gravel. The cop was still trailing him, but gaining fast. There was only one possible escape, one place the deputy could never follow.

He pulled off the lane and piloted the bike into the trees. The slalom that followed took his breath away — swerving and steering, threading the needle, bouncing over uneven ground between countless trunks.

"Kid, no!" came the cop's voice. "It's not worth it!"

Aiden set his jaw as the branches scraped his face and flailed at his body. *That's because it isn't your sister.* It was plenty worth it.

Besides, the trees were thinning out. He could see daylight just ahead. The Trek burst out of the grove — and the earth seemed to drop out from under him.

The slope was steep, the speed dizzying. By the time Aiden realized where he was, the bike was already traveling upward of forty miles per hour. Somehow, he had blundered onto the main ski slope!

The Trek kept on accelerating until he could hear the wind roaring in his ears. But he didn't dare slam on the brakes for fear of rolling, head over heels. If that happened, the best he could hope for would be a body cast.

He tried to pump the hand brake lightly, stuttering the tires. It did nothing — it was probably *supposed* to do nothing at that speed. He was too scared to steer away from directly downhill. Rough terrain could wipe him out entirely. Besides, he was already going so fast that he lacked the strength to move the handlebars in either direction.

The slope blurred as the force of gravity pulled the Trek in a screaming descent. Aiden's mind worked even more furiously than his wheels. What could he do? How might he save himself? Every passing instant ramped up his velocity. Should he jump? It seemed crazy.

But five seconds from now it'll be that much crazier because I'll be going even faster!

All he could do was hang on, struggling to keep the bike upright.

And then the blizzard hit.

Blizzard? That's impossible! Two minutes ago, there wasn't a cloud in the sky!

Yet there was no mistaking it. Ice-cold needles raked his face. Wildly blowing snow reduced visibility to zero. The Trek plowed downward through the storm. With a stab of terror, he realized he could no longer see where he was going. If he hit anything — a tree, a rock, a fence — he would be dead instantly.

It called for a split-second decision, and he made one, too quickly even to allow for a silent prayer. He coiled his body like a spring and hurled himself free of the bike.

The impact was utter devastation. If it hadn't been for the cushioning effect of the soft snow, he probably would have sustained a concussion and more than one broken bone. The momentum sent his body tumbling, and for a moment he feared that he would logroll all the way to the bottom, to crash into the wreckage of his stolen bike. But after a few seconds, he bounced to a stop in the deepening powder.

He did a quick self-exam—arms, legs, body parts. Everything seemed okay, except for the taste of blood from where he had bitten his lip. Gingerly, he got to his feet and weighed his options. The deputy was probably already on his radio, sounding the alarm. Town wasn't an option. Neither was the ski lodge at the bottom of the hill. He had to disappear and lie low until the heat was off.

He began to trudge through the driving storm until an astonishing sight met his eyes. A wheeled cart sat at the edge of the slope. On its flat back sat something that looked like a small cannon. The "blizzard" was shooting out of its barrel.

Amazed, Aiden walked out of the barrage. The sky was blue and cloudless.

A snowmaking machine!

He looked up and down the mountain. There were several others creating these wintry conditions. Wasn't it just his luck to hit the ski hill when the lodge decided to make artificial snow?

On second thought, he realized it *was* luck. Very good luck. The whiteout conditions were hiding him from the cop above and the hotel below. Twenty yards beyond the snow machine the cover of the woods beckoned.

He dropped to all fours and scooted for it.

21

On a different mountainside, thirty miles to the west, Meg sawed furiously at the ropes that bound her wrists. It was more difficult than she'd anticipated. The twine was thick, the nail file dull, the position awkward. It was almost impossible to maintain a proper grip on the manicuring tool. Drop it, and she'd be in big trouble. She had to be careful, and care took time.

Patience, she told herself.

It was hard to be patient when, at any moment, Spidey or Tiger might walk in on her. When they checked on her next, she had to be miles away.

It became a little easier once she'd worn a groove in the rope. She could feel the fibers splitting, ever so slowly, one at a time.

Keep going. This could be your last chance.

She was almost loose when there was a click, and the door opened. Petrified, she could think of nothing to do but pretend to be asleep.

Footsteps in the room. Who was it? Spidey? Tiger?

She palmed the file, praying that none of the frayed ends of twine would show. Seconds seemed like weeks.

Go away . . . go away . . . go away . . . go away . . .

At last, another click. She had passed the test, and she was alone again.

Her relief was so great that she nearly fumbled the file out of her fingers. Heart pounding, she went back to work, double speed.

The pressure of rope against skin suddenly loosened as the bonds fell away. With her hands free, she took less than a minute to untie her ankles.

In a flash, she was at the window, easing up the sash, hoisting herself silently up, over, and out. The desire to be away from the house and her captors was so strong that she sprinted through the woods, heedless of direction.

She stopped for breath only when the searing pain of her lungs would permit her not one step more. Only then did she allow the thought to enter her mind.

I have no idea where I am.

Peering through the trees at the valley below, she could not make out a single sign of life — not a house, not a road, not even power lines. She remembered the uphill slope of the ground as she'd been carried to the cabin. So downhill was the direction she had to follow.

This place was isolated, but it wasn't Antarctica. If she went far enough, sooner or later she was sure to run into somebody.

Meg prayed it would not be one of her kidnappers.

Sheriff Atkin watched a tub-sized hot cup of coffee ease through the low doorway to his office, followed by all six feet seven inches of Emmanuel Harris.

"Sit down, Agent Harris, by all means," the sheriff invited. "What can I do for the Bureau today?"

"Richard Pembleton," Harris said grimly. "Have you caught up with him yet?"

Atkin grimaced. The last thing he wanted to discuss with this fed was how a teenager had escaped from this very trailer — especially since they still had no idea how the boy had managed it. Harris was going to think he was some kind of hick.

"One of my deputies spotted him, but Pembleton gave him the slip."

The agent held out a photograph. "Is this him?"

The sheriff nodded.

"First things first," Harris told him. "That's not Richard Pembleton. He's safe at home in Maryland. The kid you're looking for is Aiden Falconer."

The name brought instant recognition from Atkin.

"*The* Aiden Falconer? But what would he be doing around here? Why should he care about Lincoln's mascot?"

"He was probably using the other boys as cover. The kid's a chameleon. He's convinced that his sister's being held around here somewhere."

The sheriff nodded. "The kidnapping. I heard about that."

Harris regarded him intently. "Any chance Aiden's onto something? Mysterious strangers? Suspicious activity?"

Atkin shrugged. "There are plenty of places to disappear in our mountains. But we're not exactly centrally located for a ransom operation. Is the Bureau planning a big play up here?"

Harris shook his head, thinking of Sorenson at the Falconer home, hopelessly entangled in rules and procedures, incapable of action. "I'm just here for Aiden. What kind of help can you give me?"

The sheriff turned to his radio. "Let's see what my deputies have turned up."

22

Under cover of the woods, Aiden made his way back up the hill. He kept the road in sight, but didn't dare show himself—not with police cars cruising the main drag every few minutes. In a town that amounted to no more than two blocks, this counted as a dragnet. He hadn't survived a daredevil thrill ride down the mountain just to get arrested on Main Street.

Yet he couldn't stay hidden forever. Meg was being held around here somewhere, maybe not too far away. He had to find her. Then the police could have him and anything else they wanted. But none of that was going to happen if he couldn't leave these woods.

His plan was to wait until dark. Surely it would be safe to come out then. He sat down on a rock, practicing his story about cousins in a green car. He was going to have to be a lot smoother than he'd been with the lady at the general store.

Dusk was falling. Soon it would be time. He hunkered down at the sound of a car, noting with relief that it wasn't a cruiser. He hadn't seen one in a while. Maybe they were giving up. After all, he wasn't exactly a fleeing murderer.

With a shiver that ran through his entire body, he realized that he was looking at the receding trunk of a green sedan.

Abandoning all caution, he burst out of the woods and hit the pavement running. In a full sprint, he tried to do the impossible — catch up to a motor vehicle. For a moment, it was working. The sedan slowed down for the two-block length of town, and Aiden actually gained on it. But then it made a sharp left onto a side road and disappeared from view.

No!

He turned on the jets, propelled by anguish and disbelief. A direct connection with his sister! So close! And now it was gone.

He barreled through town and made a left in the car's wake, struggling up a sharp grade. Desperately, his eyes raked the area. The road was steep and winding, dotted by a few small houses and ski chalets. No vehicles in the driveways; no sign of the sedan.

He forged on, refusing to be discouraged. Deep down, he knew that if the car had been heading ten miles up this road, he would never get there. And even if he did, by that time it would be so dark that he wouldn't be able to tell green from black.

"Hey, son, are you okay?"

Startled, Aiden stopped in his tracks. A man stood on the front lawn of a small cottage, rake in hand, by a mound of leaves. "Funny place to run a marathon," he observed.

"Did a green car just come by here?" Aiden panted.

The man laughed. "I've heard of *dogs* chasing cars—"

Aiden thought fast. "They left a credit card back at the gas station."

"You're looking for the Harpers'. It's a split-level stucco house about half a mile up the road, on the left." He hesitated. "Listen—when you approach the place, make sure you don't look like you're sneaking around. Their boy is just home from the service. He's an okay kid, but he's still pretty tightly wound. He saw action in Iraq. You don't want him to think you're a burglar."

"Thanks." Aiden trotted on up the street, his heart rejoicing. He recalled the terrible day—was it really less than a week ago?—when Meg had been taken. A big man, a woman, and a smaller man. Father, mother, son.

These were the people who had his sister.

He could see the house now, glowing pearl-gray stucco in the fading light. The car, a dark green Chrysler, stood in the driveway.

Aiden retreated to the cover of a small thicket of pines

across the road. He needed a strategy; he couldn't just knock on the door and ask for Meg Falconer. But calling the police wasn't an option, either. He was a wanted man in this county.

That left what? He had to break into the Harper home and see for himself if Meg was a prisoner there.

What was he — crazy? A week ago, these people had tried to kidnap him right along with her. Walking into their house would be like serving himself up on a silver platter!

It's a risk you'll have to take.

His mind made up, he hunkered down for a long wait. When the lights in the split-level went out, and the family was asleep, only then would he make his move.

Hang in there, Meg. I'm coming.

The scream that came from Spidey was barely human.

"Where is she?"

Mickey and Tiger rushed to join him in the small bedroom where Meg had been tied up. The three kidnappers found a pile of ropes, an open window, and an empty chair.

"I tied those ropes myself!" Spidey bellowed. "Look!" He held up a frayed end. "This one's been cut! How could she cut through a rope?"

"What are you staring at me for?" Mickey whined. "We were all here!"

"You were getting too friendly with that girl!" Spidey raged. "Feeding her cupcakes with candles! Were there any 'presents' at that party? Something she could have used to saw herself free?"

"No!"

"Then how did she do it?" He turned on Tiger. "You're the one who searched her. What could you have missed?"

Tiger spoke with the cold, passionless efficiency that had made her so frightening to Meg. "It doesn't matter how she got out. She's out. And every second you waste with pointless accusations, she makes it that much farther away."

Spidey bit his tongue. "Bring flashlights," he growled. "It'll be dark soon."

Mickey shrugged into his coat and followed the others into the chilly dusk. As he hurried to catch up with his accomplices, he whispered a sentence he could never let them hear:

"Good luck, Meg."

23

Huddled in the trees across from the Harper home, Aiden felt the cold for the first time. He had been coatless all day, but the wild bursts of physical exertion had kept the chill at bay. The sun had helped, too. But now it was dark. He hoped it wouldn't be too long before the family went to bed.

A terrible thought came to him: What if they didn't go to bed at all, but stood guard on Meg in shifts?

He thought back to the neighbor's warning. If the youngest Harper was "tightly wound," it probably had less to do with Iraq and more to do with the fact that there was a kidnapped girl in the house.

In the end, it didn't really matter. No circumstance, no danger, would keep Aiden from going in there.

He was so concerned with watching for signs of sleep that he was totally unprepared for what happened next. All three Harpers emerged from the front door, piled into the Chrysler, and drove away.

Aiden scrambled to adjust his thinking to this new development.

They left Meg alone. That means she's locked up, or tied up, or even unconscious . . .

In Dad's books, Mac Mulvey described houses with secret holding cells hidden behind concrete walls with doors no one could see. He could be in there, just a few feet away from her, and never know it.

I've got to act fast!

He ran across the street. Hugging the stucco wall, he slipped into the shadows of the backyard. He selected an ornamental rock out of the garden and approached the kitchen sliders. No, somewhere less obvious. His eyes traveled to the basement windows. They were small, but he was reasonably sure he could fit his long lean body through.

With a sharp blow, he broke the glass, and then tapped the loose shards from the opening. Feet first, he eased himself through the window and dropped to the basement floor.

He switched on the light and looked around. It could have been the basement of any family in America — veneer paneling, framed photos, bowling trophies, a Ping-Pong table. He scowled at the smiling pictures. A family of kidnappers! Holiday snapshots and school portraits concealing a terrible crime.

"Meg!" he hissed, throwing open doors and tapping against walls. "Meg, where are you?" Laundry room, bathroom, cedar closet — all empty.

Something wrapped around his feet, and he almost shrieked in terror. He did a mad dance, sending a fat gray tabby fleeing for the stairs.

A cat. The pounding of Aiden's heart was a jackhammer in his ears. Not a threat, except possibly to scare him to death.

He crept upstairs and checked the living room, dining room, kitchen, and a half bath. On the upper floor were three bedrooms and another bath. There was no sign of Meg. He searched every closet, opened every wardrobe, even riffled through the laundry hamper and peered into the whirlpool tub and stall shower.

In the hallway, he yanked on the cord that released a pull-down staircase leading to the attic. He climbed up, tense with anticipation. She would be here. She had to be.

He gestured blindly in the darkness until his hand found the string that turned on the light. The attic was jam-packed with luggage, cartons, and a huge array of sports equipment.

He inspected it all, poking his nose into anything large enough to conceal a prisoner. His sister was not there.

Now he had to face the terrible fact that he was wrong. Wrong about this family, their house, and their car. Meg wasn't being held here. She was miles away — maybe a lot of miles. The sighting at the general store might have been real. But everything else had been Aiden Falconer jumping to conclusions because of wishful thinking.

Along with the wave of crushing disappointment came a growing sense of horror at what he was doing this very moment. He was invading the home of an innocent family whose only crime was having three members and a green sedan.

I have to get out of here!

He crawled over a pile of fishing gear sitting in a flattened inflatable raft and began to climb down out of the attic.

It was a few seconds before he realized that there was a stocky middle-aged man standing in the hall below, gaping up at him.

"What are you doing in my house?"

Aiden reacted instantly, almost without thought. He reached up into the attic, grabbed the raft, and pulled it down onto Mr. Harper. Fishing tackle rained in all directions. As the rubber boat fell, Aiden yanked on the inflator cord. With a loud hiss, the dinghy began to fill with air, expanding into the tight hallway, pinning the man against the wall.

Aiden jumped off the attic ladder and fairly leaped down the stairs to the main floor. He was about to sprint for the front door when it opened and an unseen voice called, "Dad, is everything okay?"

He did an immediate about-face, making for the kitchen sliders.

"Johnny!" came a muffled voice from upstairs. "Call the police! There's someone in the house!"

Aiden flipped the lock and yanked on the handle. The glass door wouldn't budge. A wooden stick had been inserted in the track for extra security. He reached down to pull it out.

Running feet in the front hall. Mr. Harper's son!

The neighbor's words came back to haunt Aiden: *He saw action in Iraq. You don't want him to think you're a burglar.*

Hide!

Aiden scrambled inside the kitchen broom closet and pulled it shut in front of him. There he cowered, not daring to move, barely daring to breathe.

After everything else that had gone wrong, now he was being hunted by a trained soldier.

24

Harris was still in the sheriff's office when the call came in.

"Sheriff, it's Enid Harper on her cell phone," Janine told her boss. "She says there's an intruder in their house."

The sheriff shrugged into his coat. "I'm on my way."

"I'll go with you," put in Harris. He had a sneaking suspicion that anything unusual in this sleepy mountain town might involve Aiden Falconer.

Flashlight beams cut the darkness, playing off the black trees and underbrush.

"Margaret!" called Tiger. "Come back! You'll never survive out here all alone!" Her voice echoed in the emptiness, and there was no reply. "Nobody's going to hurt you!" she added.

"I'll hurt her," Spidey muttered darkly. "I'll wring her little neck!"

"That's not the kind of talk that's going to encourage her to turn herself in," Tiger reminded him in an annoyed tone.

"What are you mad at me for?" the big man shot back. "Why don't you ask our little friend here why he isn't exactly screaming the mountain down? Because he wants her to get away, that's why."

"That's not true!" Mickey defended himself. He wasn't sure how nervous he should be. Did Spidey truly suspect that he had helped Meg escape? Or was he just ranting and blaming, as usual? "It's just that — well — she has no flashlight. Even if she wants to come to us, maybe she can't find her way."

"Good point," Tiger approved. "One of us should be at the cabin, in case she blunders back there. Go."

Mickey trudged off, the light of his flashlight dancing ahead of him.

Spidey smacked a gloved fist against a tree trunk. "I feel like we're flying by the seat of our pants. We're being too casual about something this important!"

"What do you propose we do?" she retorted. "Burn down the forest so she's easier to find?"

"She could put us all away for a very long time!"

"Don't worry," Tiger said grimly. "Even if we don't find her, she's lost in the mountains in winter. She'll never make it out of here alive."

The broom closet was closing in on Aiden. He crouched there in total darkness, afraid to move his cramped limbs in case he touched off an avalanche of mops and brooms that would send him spilling into the kitchen.

Outside his hiding place, he could hear the two Harper men tearing the house apart, searching for him.

They'll look in the kitchen sooner or later . . .

He heard shoes on the basement steps and knew he'd never have a better opportunity to make a break for it. While they were scouring downstairs, he could remove the stick from the sliders and flee.

He eased the closet open and moved out onto the kitchen tiles. A door slammed almost directly below him. Activity in the basement. Perfect. He was home free.

He took one step. Only one.

An arm of iron closed around his neck, a knee jammed into the small of his back, and a knife—a serrated army blade—pressed up against his throat.

A harsh voice behind his ear called, "Dad—I've got him."

Aiden tried to struggle. Bad mistake. The choke hold grew stronger, and he could not breathe.

Mr. Harper ran up from the basement and took in the sight of his soldier son throttling the young intruder. "Johnny—*don't!*"

"He broke into our house, Dad!"

"He's just a kid!" his father pleaded.

Aiden fought to stay alert, as the pressure on his windpipe did not ease. The knife at his throat was terrifying. But even more frightening was the look on Mr. Harper's face. It said very plainly that he believed his son was on the verge of committing murder.

The front door was flung open, and in burst a man so tall that he had to duck his head to get past the hall fixture. The newcomer's eyes widened in shock at the drama in the kitchen.

The gun was in his big hand so quickly that no one actually saw him reach for it.

"FBI! Drop your weapon!"

The knife clattered to the floor. Johnny Harper released his captive.

Gasping, Aiden slumped to his knees. He had not believed he could ever be so happy to see Agent Emmanuel Harris.

Meg raced through the blackness of the woods, making the best of what little night sight she had. The only light came from a crescent moon and a few stars. The rest of the sky was cloud covered.

Her vision was so limited that the trees would come into view when they were only inches away — as if they were being fired at her by some maniacal video game. She threaded her way between them, bobbing and sidestepping as she fled for her life. She barely noticed the branches that slashed at her skin and the roots that bruised her ankles and tried to trip her up. Her one thought: *Escape*. She was away from her captors at last, and there was no going back, no matter what.

Earlier that night, she'd heard the kidnappers calling her name, but not for a couple of hours now.

Have I lost them? Have they given up the chase?

Meg doubted it. Anyway, she didn't intend to hang around to find out. She wouldn't be safe until she had made it to some town and marched straight into the police station.

When she stepped into the hollow, it was like the world had fallen away in front of her. A sharp pain shot up her leg as her ankle twisted. She lost her balance and pitched forward. She landed hard, her shoulder ramming into a fallen log.

No-o-o!!

The effort to keep from screaming it out loud was nearly more than she could handle.

But she was out! She was away!

Calm down!

She straightened her leg and tried to wiggle the ankle. It burned with fire but didn't seem to be broken. A sprain, nothing more.

She was lucky—this time. It would slow her down, but she could still move.

The problem isn't speed, she reflected. *It's the fact that I can't see an inch in front of me.*

Her next misstep might bring more than a simple sprain. She could break her leg or knock herself unconscious. If that happened, she might never leave these mountains. She needed a place to wait out the night, maybe catch forty winks. To rest her ankle until first light would allow her to go on her way again.

She snuggled farther into the hollow, pressing her back against the sheltering log. Now all she needed was camouflage, just in case her captors came through here.

Favoring her injured ankle, she broke boughs off a nearby pine and leaned them up against the log, forming a curtain over the hollow. Then she crawled inside, savoring the smell of pine needles. She was completely covered. The kidnappers could pass right by, and in the darkness, they would never see her.

Her ankle throbbed, and her shoe was starting to feel tight from the swelling. Even more worrisome was the thought that she had no idea how to get out of these woods, out of these mountains.

And yet the feeling of triumph and well-being would not go away.

All at once, she understood why. As of this moment, she wasn't kidnapped anymore. Lost, injured, hungry, cold — sure.

But free.

25

The first thing Agent Harris did when Aiden refused to get into the Trailblazer was to grasp him firmly by his head and one shoulder and seat him by force.

"You can't make me go home!" Aiden ranted. "I'll jump out of the car!"

So Harris handcuffed him to the inside of the door.

"You have no right to do this!" Aiden ranted. "I'm not a criminal!"

The agent looked amused. "Not unless you consider breaking and entering, stealing a bike, escaping a county lockup, and inflating a raft in a private home."

"You made that last one up!" Aiden accused.

"Maybe." Harris started the car and headed for Route 119.

Aiden struggled to keep his emotions in check. "Agent Harris, Meg is out here somewhere! Okay, not in this house. Maybe not even in this town. But in another one! The lady at the general store—"

"Saw a green car, period," Harris finished. "For all we know, it was the Harpers' car. There's no evidence that your sister is being held anywhere around here. Even if it really was her back at that mechanic's garage, they could have taken her a thousand miles west by now. Or turned south. Or north."

"So we just give up?" Aiden asked bitterly.

"We notify the authorities in the areas she's most likely to be. We update the alert with the latest information we have. Going off half-cocked doesn't help anybody — especially when it wastes FBI manpower to save your hide!"

"Nobody asked you to save my hide," Aiden muttered.

"As a matter of fact, your mother did," Harris informed him. "You know her feelings about dealing with me, but that's how worried she was. Do you have any idea what almost happened to you tonight? Can you picture what that army knife would have done to your soft little neck?"

Aiden fell silent. There was little doubt that the big agent had arrived just in time to save his life. He shivered.

"If I uncuff you," said Harris, "there's a jacket in the back. And a baseball cap that should probably go back to its rightful owner. But first you've got to promise you won't try to jump."

Aiden wouldn't answer.

The agent sighed. "Suit yourself — freeze. But you

will call your mother." He handed over his cell phone. "I promise you police brutality if you don't."

The conversation with Mom was as painful and emotionally charged as Aiden had feared. At least learning that her son was safe took a little bit of worry off her plate. She didn't ask about his adventure in the mountains, and he chose not to tell her. Besides, the only thing that really mattered was the ultimate piece of bad news — he had failed to rescue Meg.

Failed.

Aiden was glad to hear that Rufus Sehorn was still visiting the house on a regular basis to provide support. But there had been no new ransom demand received by www.bloghog.usa, and no new communication from the kidnappers. With Meg's life at risk, hearing nothing was incredibly stressful for everybody.

Aiden spoke to Dad, too. He could tell from his father's tone that Agent Sorenson was still the same gutless thumb-twiddler who had forced Aiden to run off on his own in the first place. With someone like that in charge, what chance did Meg honestly have?

This was more than a depressing ride home. It was surrender. Aiden was joining the rest of the world in giving up on his sister.

He returned the phone to his FBI rescuer. "Agent Harris — *please*! I can't leave now. There are three rest stops Meg hit that I haven't checked yet. You can come with me. Even keep me handcuffed! But I can't sacrifice the last shot at picking up her trail."

Harris tried to be kind. "Look, I want to find her, too. But there really is no trail. Besides, the National Weather Service is predicting a big blizzard for these mountains. If we don't get out, we could be stuck for days. Then, if a real lead comes in, we'll be powerless to follow it."

Aiden knew that any blizzard that might be coming could never match the storm in his tormented brain.

Aw, Meg, where are you?

26

Huddled in her meager shelter deep in the mountains, Meg Falconer peered through her pine canopy and watched a single snowflake drift to the ground. . . .

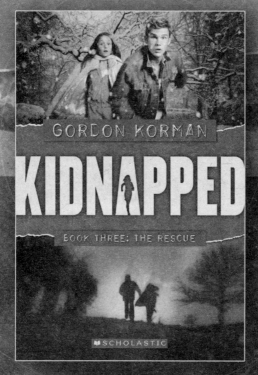

GO ON MORE THRILLING ADVENTURES WITH GORDON KORMAN!

In this suspenseful series, teens fight for survival after being shipwrecked on a desert island.

Who will be the youngest teen to climb Everest? Find out in this adventure-filled series!

In this action-packed trilogy, four young divers try to salvage sunken treasure without becoming shark bait!

Two kids become fugitives in order to clear their convicted parents' names in this heart-stopping series.